D0458298

Hockey Heat Wave

C. A. Forsyth

James Lorimer & Company Ltd., Publishers
Toronto, 1998

© 1998 C. A. Forsyth

All rights reserved. No part of this book may be reproduced or transmitted in any form or by any means, electronic or mechanical, including photocopying, or by any information storage or retrieval system, without permission in writing from the publisher.

James Lorimer & Company acknowledges the support of the Department of Canadian Heritage and the Ontario Arts Council in the development of writing and publishing in Canada. We acknowledge the support of the Canada Council for the Arts for our publishing program.

Cover illustration: Jeff Domm

Canadian Cataloguing in Publication Data

Forsyth, C.A. (Christine A.)
  Hockey heat wave
  (Sports stories)

ISBN 1-55028-619-6 (bound)   ISBN 1-55028-618-8 (pbk.)

I. Title. II. Series: Sports stories (Toronto, Ont.)
PS8561.06966H6 1998   jC813'.54   C98-930352-7
PZ7.F66Ho 1998

James Lorimer & Company Ltd.,
Publishers
35 Britain Street
Toronto, Ontario
M5A 1R7

Distributed in the United States
by: Orca Book Publishers
P.O. Box 468
Custer, WA U.S.A.
98240-0468

Printed and bound in Canada

Contents

1	Huntsville Here We Come	1
2	Stick Around	6
3	Paddling for Points	13
4	Boot Camp	20
5	Splish, Splash, Slash	26
6	Blood and Ice	33
7	Camp Clown	39
8	Minor Improvement	44
9	Night Crawlers	51
10	Dog Day Afternoon	58
11	Trouble Afoot	63
12	Truth and Consequences	70
13	Making Up for Lost Goals	75

For my dad, Ken,
from his number one fan

1

Huntsville Here We Come

Separate cabins." With two words, the camp director dashed my hopes that summer hockey camp was going to be the best experience of my life.

"NO!" My response boomed in the tiny log cabin that served as the camp office. The director, Mary Skorsgaard, frowned, and deep lines creased her face. My dad put his hand on my shoulder and began to speak, but I interrupted him. "Why *can't* Zack and I be in the same cabin?"

"It's all part of the camp experience, Mitch," Mary replied. "We think it's important for you to get to know the rest of the campers, and to make new friends."

"I don't need any new friends," I grumbled.

"Mitch!" Mom exclaimed, with her best "I am so disappointed in you" look.

"Sorry." I looked at my best friend, Zack, for support. Zack doesn't say much around adults, and this situation had him completely mute. I nudged him, hoping to prompt a verbal reaction. He just stood there like a buzz-cut totem pole, with a scowl on his face.

Mary apparently decided the matter was settled and started going through papers with Mom and Dad. I decided to join my friend in a bout of serious sulking.

Okay, I guess I didn't have anything to whine about. There I was, with my best friend, at a Muskoka hockey camp for two whole weeks in July.

Let me introduce myself. I'm Mitch Stevens. I'm thirteen, I live in Toronto, and Zack and I play hockey with the Hillcrest Stingers.

Back in March, we were almost enemies — after twelve years of being best friends — all because of a big misunderstanding that involved our coach, who is also my dad. But we worked out our differences and were lucky enough to win two spots at a special hockey camp.

It was the second Saturday in July, and my parents had decided to drive us to camp and stay overnight at my Aunt Barb's house in Huntsville. Once we passed Steeles Avenue on the 400, the traffic moved quickly. Dad was right into his stories about playing junior hockey, back when pucks were square.

Zack and I were having a great season, skating together on the A-line for the Stingers. I play centre and Zack is right wing. Our team was at the top of its league and we were hot. Then two things happened. First, our coach, Mr. Minelli, announced that the top twenty-five players in our league would be chosen, along with fifteen kids from other leagues, to go to a special summer hockey camp. Then Mr. Minelli got transferred to Halifax and my dad took over as coach.

I thought it was going to be great having Dad as our coach, but things didn't exactly work out the way I expected. Within a few weeks I wound up on the B-line with the underachievers, and Zack and I ended up as bitter enemies. It wasn't fun, but we worked things out.

And there we were, on our way to hockey camp with thirty-eight of the best players in Ontario.

* * *

Have you ever been to Huntsville? It's north of Toronto, in Muskoka, which is called cottage country because it's full of lakes and a lot of people from the city have cottages up there. The lakes have funny names like Mary and Fairy. Fortunately, our camp wasn't on one of those. Camp Lone Pine isn't actually in Huntsville, it's in Baysville, on Lake of Bays. Pretty original, eh? When we got the brochures, Zack misread it and told everybody at school that we were going to a camp on Lake of Boys. No girls allowed.

The road was winding, with lots of hills. I could tell Dad was enjoying the drive. He was appreciating it so much he drove right past the entrance to the camp.

The sign for Camp Lone Pine had a big picture of a fake-looking pine tree, with a really fake-looking sun beside it. The reason the pine tree looked so artificial, was because there were plenty of real ones in the woods all around it. It didn't look too lonely to me.

A gravel driveway ran downhill from the road. It had deep ruts in it, and Dad had to drive the van carefully to avoid the bigger ones. The road widened into a large clearing where a bunch of cars were parked. On our right was a small log building. Farther down the hill was a much bigger log building, and if you looked through the trees you could see the water.

"Hey, Zack," I said. "Check out the trees." Everywhere you looked were trees, and most of them were pines.

"Yeah," Zack said, laughing. "I wonder which one is the lonely one."

"I'm sure there's a good explanation for why the camp is named Lone Pine," Mom said.

"Maybe the name Thousand Pines was taken," Dad joked as he put the van in park. "Okay, everybody out. And watch out for pine trees!"

We trooped into the small office and were greeted by Mary, who is probably the tallest woman I've ever seen. Her hair was white blond and her pale iceberg eyes made me think she might have been an alien. She looked pretty old to me, but she had muscular arms and legs.

And that brings us back to Zack and me sulking in the camp office. I was just starting to chill out when I heard two more words that put the icing on the puck.

"Eddie Genova." Zack was looking out the screen door into the parking area. "Eddie's here."

Eddie Genova. Rangers' winger. Ace scorer. Arch rival. Eddie and his dad were headed our way. I've never seen Eddie without a hat or a helmet, and as he marched toward us I noticed his big head looked odd. When he got closer, I realized that the black baseball cap he was wearing backwards was the same colour as the wild-looking hair sticking out from underneath it.

I heard a chair scrape against the floor as Mary said, "There, you see? You already know someone in your cabin."

My head snapped around. "Eddie's in *my* cabin?" My jaw was headed for the floor.

"No," she replied. "He's in Zack's cabin."

I looked at Zack for a reaction. He just shrugged. The fact is, Zack never had the kind of trouble I'd had with Eddie. Zack's a big guy, not too tall, but solidly built and there aren't many kids in our league who can push him around on the ice. Eddie's even bigger than Zack, which means he's a fair bit bigger than me. I'm more on the lean side. In other words, Eddie leans on me a lot. He's run me into the boards so often, Zack started calling him the Lord of the Boards. Ask me how many layers of paint there are on the boards in any arena we play in. Believe me, I know.

Eddie marched into the office with his usual swagger, banging the screen door against the wall. "I heard you guys were coming." He turned his beady brown eyes on me. "How ya doin', runt?"

2

Stick Around

I was happy to get out of the office, even if it was to check out our separate cabins and dump our stuff. Zack and I walked silently behind my parents as they chattered like the hosts of a nature show. The path to our cabins wound down through the trees, toward the lake. Zack's cabin, Sycamore, was only about thirty metres from Alder, where I was bunking.

A clanging bell told us that it was time to get down to business. With nothing more than a quick glance around my four-person cabin, I headed back up the hill with Zack to board a bus for the Huntsville arena.

The parking lot was jammed with kids and parents. With everybody wandering around, it was hard to tell how many kids were campers. Zack and I retrieved our big equipment bags and sticks from the back of my parents' van and put them in a growing pile beside one of two yellow school buses.

A young guy, wearing a black T-shirt with the name "Steve" embroidered above the words "Assistant Hockey Coach," directed us to board the first bus. We said a hasty goodbye to Mom and Dad, but they didn't appear as sorry to see me go as I thought they should have been.

I boarded behind Zack, giving my name to the driver as I stepped in. As he turned into the aisle, Zack stopped short, leaving me no opportunity to avoid crashing into him. We nearly toppled into two girls sitting in the first row of seats. They snickered as we lurched toward the back of the bus.

"Did you see that?" Zack whispered.

"Hey, I'm sorry. You stopped too fast," I said, dumbly.

"No, the girls. There are girls here!" Zack hissed.

"Yeah, what's up with that?" I replied, perplexed. I had assumed that the hockey camp would be just for guys.

There weren't any seats left for us to sit in together, so Zack settled in beside Eddie Genova. I looked around. The only seat left was beside one of the guys I'd met just a few minutes ago in my cabin. I didn't want to sit with him, because I couldn't remember his name, but I sat down anyway. Huntsville was about twenty minutes away. I'd look pretty stupid standing all the way back to town.

He was a kid about my size, not big like Zack and Eddie. Dark brown hair stuck out from under his baseball cap. I kept my mouth shut, trying to avoid conversation.

"I'm Doug, from your cabin, remember?" He looked at me, and then glanced away. There was one of those awkward pauses where I remained mute. "I feel kinda stupid. I don't remember your name," he said finally, breaking the ice.

"Mitch Stevens," I replied, relieved. "How ya doin'?"

"I'm no good with names. On our team, everybody has nicknames. I'm Pizza Boy, because my sister works at the pizza place where we go after games."

I wasn't sure what that had to do with hockey, but we chatted comfortably. I discovered that Doug was from Huntsville, which came as a surprise, because I thought the camp was only for kids from around Toronto.

"You're kidding, right?" he said, when I told him. "We're here for the *Ontario* select team, you know."

"Right, I knew that," I replied, somewhat embarrassed.

"Ontario isn't just Toronto, you know," Doug said. I thought he might have been ticked off, but he was smiling as he said it.

The trip to Huntsville and the Centennial Centre took nearly thirty minutes. We spilled out of the bus only to wait impatiently for the equipment bus to arrive. While we waited, Doug showed Zack and me around the building. I don't think I've ever seen an arena with a swimming pool in it. It was a decent place, with the usual photos of old hockey players on the walls. The Centennial Centre's pretty new, so none of the old guys in the pictures ever played there. They have a new junior team in Huntsville, and Doug spoke as proudly of them as though he played on the team himself.

When the bags arrived, we filed down the corridor to the dressing rooms. We were told to look for a locker with our name on it. Our stuff would stay at the arena for the next two weeks so we wouldn't need two buses each day.

When I found my locker, there was already somebody suiting up next to it. I glanced at the thin kid with reddish brown curly hair. He looked familiar.

"Hi, Mitch," he said, pleasantly. "Pretty weird being on the same team, eh?"

"Totally," I agreed, while rapidly scanning my brain for his name. He took a goalie's mask out of his bag and jammed it on his head, laughing.

"Brian Epstein. I almost didn't recognize you without your mask on," I laughed, relieved.

Brian was the goalie for the Eagles. We called him the Wizard, because he could make scoring opportunities disappear into thin air. I wasn't too sure I liked the idea of Epstein getting any better. I had enough trouble scoring against him as it was.

"I saw you and Zack Andermann on the bus," Brian said, "and a few others from our league. Looks like it could be fun, eh?"

I've never had much reason to talk to Brian. I'm usually too busy firing pucks at his head. He seemed like a nice guy, though, which is more than I could say for Eddie Genova, who was over in the opposite corner impatiently banging his stick against his locker door.

* * *

There were five coaches, which, if I counted right, meant one for every eight kids. They hustled us onto the ice, and for the first time, it felt odd to be in skates — because it was July, I guess.

A pile of practice pucks littered centre ice. Whooping with enthusiasm, we hit the ice like a tornado, fighting for a disk. There were two goalies per net and they jostled for control of the creases. It was chaos, and it was awesome fun.

I scooped a puck from one of the girls, which gave me a guilty satisfaction. I hogged it, looping around the ice, looking for Zack. Finally, I spotted him peppering Brian and another goalie with rebound shots. The two goalies were getting in each other's way, letting the puck bounce back into play repeatedly. Zack was grinning from ear to ear.

"Just like hitting a tennis ball against a wall," he crowed, as I skated up with my own puck. "Give it a shot, Mitch," he encouraged.

I pinged one off the post, losing the puck to another skater. Zack laughed, then passed another one over to me. My next shot hit Brian's skate and popped back to me like it was on a string.

"You're right," I said, taking another shot as the two goalies separated to face attacks from their quarters. The puck strolled into the net. My first goal at hockey camp, coming three minutes into the festivities.

The inevitable whistle put an end to the hijinks. The coaches herded us to centre ice, where we faced them in a loose semicircle.

The big cheese was a tall, squarely built guy, who looked like he was around my dad's age, which I think is thirty-eight. He said we could call him Stan. As far as I could tell, he wasn't anybody famous in hockey.

Stan introduced the other coaches, who circulated through us, handing out plastic ID holders on strings. The IDs were about ten centimetres square and had each player's name, position and the name and location of his or her home team. They told us we should wear them for the next few days until we got to know each other. I was really relieved. Now I wouldn't look like such a fool because I couldn't remember my cabin mates' names.

"All right, kids," Stan said, "listen up. There are forty of you here for the next two weeks. You're going to work harder than you ever have. At the end of the two weeks, only twenty-five will be chosen for the Ontario select team."

My jaw dropped to the ice. I looked at Zack, who appeared equally shocked. Stan was still talking, but I didn't hear another word. Only twenty-five out of forty! I thought we were already on the select team. I looked around at the other kids, but nobody was grumbling or asking questions.

Zack nudged Eddie, who was standing next to him. "I thought we were already on the team," he said quietly.

"You're kidding, right?" Eddie sneered, looking past Zack, straight at me. "It was in the stuff they sent. They invited forty kids, and they'll select twenty-five." His beady black eyes bored into me. "Can't you guys read?"

The real workout was about to begin, so we were saved from having to admit we hadn't read the material. As we followed Stan's orders and skated to the end of the rink, I was feeling pretty stupid. When the packages had arrived from hockey camp, we opened them together, threw out the "Dear Camper" letters, kept the colour brochures and gave our parents the "Dear Parent/Guardian" stuff. I'll admit, we didn't read the brochures either. My confidence took a sudden dip.

"Anybody here have a heart condition?" Stan chuckled. We were lined up two deep in front of the goal. "First row, go!" Stan roared to the accompaniment of a whistle. Twenty kids made a mad dash to the other end of the rink where two coaches waited on opposite sides of the goal line. Zack was the first one to cross the line. I waited in the second group for Stan to give the signal.

At the whistle, I dug in and pumped furiously to the other end. Unlike Zack, I wasn't first, more like mid-pack, but certainly not last. As soon as we got there, the coaches sent the first line back for another try. I couldn't tell if Zack was first again, because they sent my group up while Zack's group was still skating. After the fourth sprint I was starting to fade, and on the fifth and final sprint, I arrived second to last. I freaked.

If it was speed and endurance they were looking for, I was doomed. I'm not a breakaway guy, that's Zack's job. I'm more of a playmaker. I play centre and I'm pretty quick with the stick.

The pucks were back on the ice and I was itching to get at them. Stick work, stick work, I prayed silently. Let's get into some stick work.

"You guys still alive?" Stan asked, grinning. I was starting to dislike Stan. But a moment later, he turned into my saviour. "Centres and forwards line up over there," he gestured to his left. "Defencemen and goalies stay on this side."

Zack and I skated the short distance to the centre line where pucks were lined up a half metre apart.

"You know what to do," said Steve. "Pick it up and carry it to the other end. Shoot from the point."

Zack and I chose our places so we would skate together. When our turn came, we looked over at each other, nodded solemnly and attached the pucks. Zack was faster, and a little smoother, but we both carried our pucks efficiently, switching them easily from the front to the back of our sticks. Zack got to the point and unloaded a big shot that found the centre of the net.

I was right behind him. I got my shot off quickly and cleanly, but my angle wasn't quite as good as Zack's. The puck hit the post on the way in, but the momentum was greater than the deflection and it stayed in the net. I was relieved.

Watching the rest of the players, I began comparing myself with them. It was a strange feeling. We weren't on a team anymore, it was just Zack and me against thirty-eight rival players.

3

Paddling for Points

The bus had barely bumped to a stop in the camp parking lot before kids vaulted through the doors. Tearing down the hill like wild animals, we raced for our cabins. The door to Alder was open because two of my bunkies were already in there, tearing off their clothes. By the time the six of us raced out, headed for the lake in our swimsuits, it looked like a clothing bomb had gone off in our cabin. We didn't care, we were hot, and totally psyched up for a cool dip in Lake of Bays.

Lots of kids, both boys and girls, were already swimming or hanging out at the beach. I counted a lot more than the hockey players I had expected to find in the water. I asked Doug about the other kids, and he told me that they were at Lone Pine for soccer camp. There must have been a hundred people splashing around. I didn't wait for Zack, the water was too inviting.

I wasn't in the water two minutes when Zack came splashing vigorously up to me.

"Check it out," he said, pointing into the lake behind me.

"Holy cow," I exclaimed. On the tiniest island I've ever seen, about a hundred metres from shore, was a single skinny pine tree. "It's the lonely pine! I've gotta call my mom!" Instead of a reply, Zack dunked me. I came up swinging, but I was pretty much alone. The rest of the kids were halfway to shore, heading toward Steve, the assistant hockey coach, who was blowing his whistle and waving his arms.

By the time I got to shore, Steve had been joined by one of the other coaches. The crowd was getting rowdy again, but Steve silenced us with an ear-splitting whistle. "Listen up, campers," he said. "We've got four paddleboats and two nets. Two people per boat and one goalie. Cabin against cabin. Do I have any volunteers?"

My hand shot up like a rocket. Zack's was right up there too. Hands were going up all over. Steve pointed at Zack, "What's your cabin," he said.

Zack looked around sheepishly. "Um, it's sick something," he said, turning to Eddie. "Help me out here, eh? I'm drowning."

"Sycamore!" Eddie shouted, amid hoots of laughter.

I checked with Doug, "Ours is Alder, right?"

"You got it," he said, still waving his arms like a windmill. He was pretty difficult to ignore, considering that he was the only one with his hands still up.

"Slow down there, Doug," Steve said. "You'll be too pooped to participate. What's your cabin?"

Four voices shouted in unison, "Alder!"

Beside me, Zack grumbled, "You got an easy one."

Steve led us over to four blue paddleboats. Each boat had two seats, a little steering wheel, and two sets of pedals like a bicycle. They were sitting on the sand, and Steve instructed us to pick them up and carry them to the water.

I was surprised to see how light they were. As we stood in the water beside our boats, Steve explained the rules. The rest of the hockey campers clustered around to listen. The soccer players, who had already had their turns on the paddleboats, arranged themselves on the beach to watch the show.

"The red goal is the Alder goal, the blue one is the Sycamore goal," he explained, pointing to two goal nets floating at either end of a swimming area bounded by floating plastic buoys. "One player drives, the other shoots. You can use your paddle or your feet, no hands. Try to stay in your boat, no high sticking, no ramming. That's it," he said.

While it felt quite natural to pair up with Doug, I felt a twinge of jealousy when I saw Zack and Eddie sharing some laughs together.

We waded into the water, to raucous shouts from the spectators. "I'll drive," Doug said, climbing awkwardly into the boat. It dipped precariously, threatening to dump him back into the water. I leaned on the other side, to balance his weight, and slithered aboard like a snake. The other two guys in our cabin didn't have as much trouble getting their boat going.

Paddling was easy, just like riding a bike, but the boats didn't move very fast and they turned very slowly. The face-off was going to be fun. The shooters in the boats would be using a paddle instead of a hockey stick. I snatched one up from Steve, who was standing hip-deep in the water. The two goalies were splashing their way to the goals, each with plastic floats around their waists. Steve waded in until the water was up to his armpits, carrying a big striped beach ball. He pointed to a spot around the centre of the "rink." As soon as the four boats were in position around the imaginary face-off circle, Steve blew a whistle and tossed the ball between the boats.

Doug and I paddled like maniacs toward the ball, bumping the other boats, despite Steve's warning. The ball squirted out between our boat and Zack's.

"Turn left," I shouted. "Turn left!" Doug cranked the wheel hard but the boat's progress was slow. We came alongside Zack's boat, moving in opposite directions. Eddie let out a war whoop and swung his paddle like a golf club. Instead of connecting with the beach ball, he whacked my paddle with sufficient force to knock me out of the boat. I came up sputtering, only to see Zack and Eddie drive off toward our goal, in control of the ball.

My boat was three metres away from me. "Come back," I shouted, in frustration. "Back up!"

"I can't," Doug shouted back. "You'll have to swim faster!" Meanwhile, Eddie shot the ball squarely into the net. Steve whistled a stop, and Eddie retrieved the ball from the goalie. They paddled back to the face-off area, while I swam like mad to get back to my boat. I was still in the water, between Zack and Eddie's boat and the face-off.

"Look, it's another ball!" Eddie said, ominously waving his paddle around my head.

"Take it easy, Eddie," Zack said. "Be careful."

"Sorry, Zack. It looked like another bag of hot air," Eddie replied, chopping the water with the paddle.

"I heard that!" I shouted after him. By the time I got back into my boat, I was in a rage. "Hurry up," I urged Doug. "We'll miss the face-off!"

"Chill out, Mitch," Doug said, calmly. "We've got another boat out here. We're a team."

Team, schmeam. On my team, it was always Zack and me — playing *against* Eddie Genova.

The ball was already in play, in the control of our cabin-mates. Doug and I hollered to let them know we were ready. We were closer to the Sycamore goal, so they bounced it our way. As the ball drifted near, I realized I'd lost my paddle when I went into the water. Unaccustomed to using my feet to propel an object, I accidentally hoofed the ball right into Zack and Eddie's boat.

Our teammates screamed, "No hands, no hands!" Zack and Eddie were killing themselves trying to get the ball out of their boat with their legs and feet, but they kept bumping it back and forth between them like a pinball. I laughed so hard I couldn't paddle.

When the ball finally arrived back into play, it was about a metre and a half in front of our boat on Doug's side. Zack bore down on it, while Eddie swept his paddle back and forth over the water.

There was no way Doug could swing the boat enough to put the ball on my side. "Go for it," I said to him.

"Take the wheel," he commanded. Doug stuck his leg out, waving it in a silly parody of Eddie. We were awfully close together, and for a minute I thought Eddie might whack him with his paddle, but Doug got some leg on the ball and managed to boot it out of Eddie's reach.

"Oh, noooo!" I heard Doug scream in mock horror. In the background, hoots of laughter rose from the crowd. I looked up to see the ball skimming toward our own goal. Brian paddled like a demon in his float, catching the ball easily. He tossed it out toward our teammates who whacked it up the "ice" toward the opposing goal.

By that time, Doug and I had managed to get our boat turned around and headed in the right direction. Paddling furiously, we passed two boats and were right behind Zack and Eddie in hot pursuit of the ball.

"Duh duh, duh duh ...!" I chanted, imitating the theme from *Jaws*. Doug joined in the chant.

"Eddieeee!" Doug squealed. "Don't go in the water, Eddieee!" I could hear the swooshing of the two other boats close behind. Their goalie was bobbing and waving about a metre in front of the net. We drew even with Zack's boat, the ball between us. I got off a clean shot, but the goalie deflected it with his head.

Fortunately, he sent it our way. And even more fortunately, he splashed down in the opposite direction, leaving the goal wide open. We plowed the blunt bow of the boat into the ball, pushing it slowly toward the open net.

"Is it okay to score this way?" Doug inquired casually, as I steered the ball.

"Beats me," I replied.

"Maybe you should kick it or something," he said.

"Okay," I answered.

"Just try to stay in the boat this time, Mitch."

"No problemo," I said, drawing my knee up to my chin.

Doug steered off to the left, letting the ball float free on my side. We were practically in the net, and the goalie was centimetres from getting his clutches on the ball. I booted the sphere, lifting it out of the goalie's reach.

"He sco … " my words were cut short by a bump from behind that dumped me back into the water, and sent our boat into the net.

Steve splashed over to extricate Doug from the goal, and I joined him. Over my shoulder I could see Zack and Eddie laughing their heads off. I guessed they thought it was funny, sending me swimming for the second time. I glared at Eddie and let my eyes rest on Zack a moment. It was just a game, I knew that. But best friends never laugh at each other. That's a rule.

I guess I got tired from all that swimming around, because on the next face-off, the ball squirted right by me into the clutches of Zack and Eddie. We gave chase but the two bigger guys had no trouble outpaddling us. Zack had one hand on the wheel, and one foot on the ball. His shot was straight and true. Brian Epstein, the Wizard, had lost his magic. Seconds later, Steve ended the play and called for the next two teams.

* * *

Back on the beach, Zack called me over to where he and Eddie were sitting. I joined them reluctantly, still feeling betrayed.

"Great game, eh?" Zack enthused.

"For you, maybe," I said, rather sulkily.

"Ah, get over it," Eddie interjected. "You were beat by a superior force."

I looked at him, sitting so smugly beside my lifelong friend. "Yeah, right," I replied, lamely. Some hours later, I was sure I would think of the perfect come back. In the meantime, I parked beside Zack and listened to Eddie give a blow-by-blow of the next match.

Zack cuffed him on the shoulder. "Shut up, Eddie, I can't concentrate."

I wished I'd said that.

4

Boot Camp

Our first full day at camp started with breakfast in the dining hall, where we kept up a loud rivalry with the soccer players. We didn't get to linger long over the eggs and bacon, though, before Stan blew the whistle and we stampeded to the bus.

Zack and Eddie and their other bunkmates hung together during the half-hour ride, which kind of bugged me. It wasn't that I didn't like the guys in my cabin. I mean, Doug was turning out to be pretty decent. I just didn't have any time to talk to Zack without Eddie and his other bunkies around, and I was starting to feel left out.

I was pretty anxious to get back onto the ice to show Stan and the other coaches what I could do, so I wasted no time getting dressed at the arena. Stan explained the daily program to us. We would have two hours of drills in the morning, break for lunch for an hour, come back for a classroom session, hit the ice for one more hour and then head back to camp for leisure activities. It sounded like a pretty slack program.

We started with stretching and warm-ups. Zack grumbled behind me, echoing my own thoughts. We hate stretching, especially since one of the girls said it was just like warming up for ballet. Yuck. Once the coaches figured we had stretched enough, we did some laps around the rink.

On the fourth round, we had to pick a puck off the boards and fire it back to one of the coaches. At first, I overskated the puck. Embarrassed, I stopped, ready to make a second try. "Keep skating, Mitch," Stan called out. "Get it on the next round."

By the time I got moving, three players had passed me. "New stick?" Eddie's jeering voice came from behind me.

My temper flared instantly, and while I was mentally composing a brilliant comeback, Eddie fell flat on his face.

"Hey!" Eddie shouted in indignation. I glanced back to see Doug grinning broadly. I don't know what happened, but I appreciated the gesture.

"New skates?" I gleefully called back to Eddie. I flashed Doug a grin, and got my head back into the drill. On the next pass, I connected with the puck, but shot wide of Steve's waiting stick. Fortunately, Eddie was still at the opposite end, so I was spared his commentary on my lousy shot.

A whistle ended the warm-up before I had another pass. The real business of hockey camp was about to begin. We were split into three groups — forwards, defence and goalies. Forwards and defence would work together part of the time, and then separate to practise skills specific to their positions. The four goalies had one coach to themselves, concentrating their drills at one end. That left the rest of the rink for the other thirty-six of us.

"Send in the cones!" Stan shouted, as the assistant coaches skated onto the ice carrying a stack of orange pylons. They placed three rows of four pylons across the width of ice, while Stan split us into three groups of twelve. I was in group two, Zack and Doug in group three, and Eddie in group one.

The assistant coach for my group was named Chuck. It wasn't long before I decided that he was a bit of a jerk. He demonstrated the drill for us, skating all the way around each pylon in a figure eight pattern. One of the six girls on the ice, Caitlin, put up her hand and asked, "With or without sticks?"

Chuck replied, "This is hockey, kid, not figure skating." Stan overheard Chuck's remark and shot him a look. Meanwhile, Caitlin defended herself by pointing out that Chuck had demonstrated without a stick.

I took a good look at Caitlin. She seemed pretty confident, especially in the way she looked Chuck straight in the eye. She was a bit shorter than me, and under her helmet I could see blond hair plastered to her forehead.

The exchange between Caitlin and Chuck started a round of snickering which brought Stan over. After a brief summit between the two coaches, Chuck skated away to oversee group one, leaving us with Stan. I was very relieved. Of all our coaches, I liked Stan the best.

He retrieved his stick from the ice and beckoned Caitlin saying, "Come on. Let's show them how it's done."

Caitlin hustled over to Stan and then followed him around the pylons, moving her stick back and forth in front of her, imitating Stan. They reached the opposite side where Stan gave a short blast of his whistle to get the rest of us going.

There was much bumbling as we formed into a line, with me at the head. I glided confidently toward the first pylon, and executed the sweep quite cleanly. Unfortunately, changing direction I crashed into the next one, forcing it out of line and bringing the first round of laughter from my mates.

"Keep going, Mitch," Stan called, skating up to replace the cone and signal the next player. I was happy to make it to the end of the line without further mishap. I was happier still to see that I wasn't the only one to bump into the pylons.

While we waited for the rest of the skaters, there was a fair bit of grumbling from the ranks. "I think they're too close together," Caitlin said, having watched the rest of us skate.

"That's not it," I said. "They've got magnets in them that pull our skates."

Caitlin scrunched up her face with a dubious look. "I don't think so," she said.

"It's true," I continued. I read about it in the brochures. They've got this force field, and you've got to be super accurate to avoid getting sucked in." I was on a roll.

"Is that what happened to you?" she demanded. "You ran straight into one."

"I was just being a bit lazy," I replied. "It won't happen again." Yeah, you wish, I thought.

"That is the stupidest thing I ever heard," Caitlin said, emphatically. "You're making it up."

Instead of answering, I just smiled. It could be true. At least it would explain my goof-up.

On the next go, Stan had us take pucks and weave between the pylons. Feeling confident, I took my turn swinging onto the course, in control. I executed the first S-turn, smoothly shifting the puck from the front to the back of my stick. I decided to turn up the heat, and put a little more speed into it. The increased speed forced me to make wider turns, and I had to work harder with the puck.

It was going great until the last turn, when the puck squirted away toward group one. I had to make a ninety degree turn to chase it, and, as luck would have it, Eddie was just starting a run down his own line and my puck and his puck seemed drawn together by some invisible force.

"Stevens," he shouted in annoyance, "get out of my way!" Eddie batted my puck with entirely unnecessary force, sending it bouncing off the opposite board. The puck shot into the net behind an unsuspecting goalie. "Interception!" Eddie crowed. "Genova scores!"

I glared at Eddie, whacking my stick on the ice in frustration. Stan waved me back into line, but Eddie still had a few words for me.

"You're such a loser, Stevens," he hissed. I whirled around in a fury, ready to tear Eddie's head off, but Stan suddenly materialized between us.

"That's enough, Eddie," he said, gently pushing me away. I skated away reluctantly, curious to hear what Stan was saying to Eddie as they continued to talk. Sometimes it's hard to see people's expressions behind the cages on their helmets, but to me it looked like Eddie wasn't smiling anymore.

By the time lunch came around I was ready for a break. Zack and I grabbed a box lunch from a row of hampers outside the dressing rooms, and headed outside for some Muskoka sunshine. Doug joined us, and we ate while enjoying the view of the river below.

"Why does that guy Eddie give you such a hard time?" Doug asked.

"It's not a big deal," I said, defensively. "It doesn't bother me."

"Yeah, but he's all over you," Doug continued. "What did you ever do to him?"

Zack, who had been pretty quiet up to that point, said, "Eddie's not so bad. It's just the way he is. He likes to give Mitch a hard time. Mitch doesn't care, do you Mitch?"

Actually, I did care. Who needs some guy busting you when you're trying to snag one of twenty-five spots on a select team? During the regular season, I only saw Eddie for sixty minutes every few weeks. Now I had him in my face for two whole weeks. "Nah, I don't care," I replied.

"TV time," Zack said, looking over at the doors of the Centennial Centre where kids were heading back in for the afternoon classroom session.

We were among the last of the players to arrive and there weren't a lot of spare chairs in the crowded room. Zack, Mr. Friendly, spied a couple of spots beside Eddie and dragged me over.

Contrary to what Zack thought, "TV time" was work of a different sort. We really had to pay attention as Stan explained the theory, strategy and mechanics of the game. I could see that Zack's attention was drifting. He was like that in school. Eddie's brow was furrowed in concentration and he jiggled his feet annoyingly.

The way Stan explained the game reminded me of playing chess with Dad. It was all thinking ahead, planning your moves and reacting to your opponent. I was almost sorry we had to go back onto the ice.

The afternoon ice session was mercifully short. Day two and I was already feeling the burn. Fortunately, I wasn't the only one. When Eddie fanned an easy shot, I took a shot of my own. "What's the matter, Genova? The puck too hot for you?"

Eddie threw a black look my way. Suddenly, a grin popped out on his face, a split second before I flipped backwards into the net.

5

Splish, Splash, Slash

We dragged ourselves onto the bus, moaning and groaning, all the way back to camp.

"I need a rest, man," Eddie had said, slouching in his seat. "If they keep working us like that for two weeks, I'm going home in a box."

Grunts of agreement rose from the overheated ranks, as the air in the bus grew hotter. Zack was sitting beside me in the back, with a wet T-shirt wrapped around his head like a turban. His face was bright red.

"Not me," he said. "I'm going to swim out to the lonely pine and look for turtles."

"What turtles?" I asked, my interest aroused.

"I don't know, any old turtles," he replied.

"How do you know there are turtles out there?" I continued.

"If there aren't, there should be," Zack answered, illogically.

"In other words, you don't know if there are turtles or not," I said. Zack just shrugged, closed his eyes and leaned his head back. "Tell you what," I said, "you swim out there. If you find turtles, put some in your shorts and bring them back to shore."

"Better not be snapping turtles," Doug joked. The kids around us laughed, and soon the joke had spread through the bus. A few kids started chanting, "Snap, snap, snap!" to a chorus of laughter. Zack's face got a little redder, but he was still smiling.

By the time the bus got to camp, our energy was restored. As Zack stepped off the bus, Caitlin snapped her fingers, starting a round of giggles from the rest of the girls standing by the door.

"Thanks, buddy," Zack said, giving me a light punch in the shoulder.

"Any time, Zack, any time," I replied, with a poorly concealed smirk and a very small twinge of guilt. I had a feeling that the little joke might haunt Zack for the rest of our stay.

We didn't waste any more time heading for the beach. Even Eddie was energized enough to hit the water. It seemed the soccer players had a head start on us — their bodies littered the beach.

"D'ya see that dock over there?" Eddie asked, pointing toward a long, narrow wooden dock that jutted into the deeper water.

"Yeah," Zack and I answered in unison. We waited for Eddie to continue, but he just smiled and stripped off his T-shirt.

"Nothing wrong with your eyesight," he laughed, heading in that direction. We looked at each other, shaking our heads. Eddie still had his hat on. When he reached the shore end of the dock, he stopped, squared his shoulders and let out an ear-splitting yell. "Cowabunga!" Eddie ran like a demon for the end of the dock, his arms windmilling. Without stopping he launched himself off the end of the platform, his knees tucked up to his chest. He landed with an atomic-sized splash about two metres from the end of the dock. His cap drifted toward shore.

I looked at Zack, he looked at me. We took off for the dock. Zack may be faster on skates, but on sand, I was metres ahead by the time he got there. I tore to the end, timing my leap perfectly. My brilliantly executed cannonball splashed down a good kilometre farther into the lake than Eddie's. Well, maybe just half a metre. But farther.

I broke the surface in time to see Zack land between me and the dock. The bigger they are, the shorter the distance they fly. Eddie was making big splashy tracks for the shore.

"Caitlin!" I shouted as she floated by on an inflatable raft. "Caitlin, wake up!"

"I am awake!" she shouted back, annoyed. "What do you want, Mitch?"

"We need you to judge our contest," I said. "Please." Caitlin looked like the kind of person who would appreciate polite requests.

"What contest?" Despite her annoyance, Caitlin paddled over to where I was treading water. I explained the game to her and she agreed to be our judge. Eddie was already into his second run as I headed for shore.

Zack waited long enough for Eddie to resurface and clear away from the end of the runway before he stepped onto the dock. A crowd was lining up behind him, ready to get into the game. With a joyful whoop, Zack leaped into action.

I could see that Zack's distance was better than Eddie's. Caitlin, now sitting astride her float, paddled into position parallel to where Zack entered the water. She was getting into it now. Her right hand was raised, its palm facing the shore to indicate that the next contestant was to hold. Once Zack was out of range, Caitlin dropped her arm and another kid, a soccer player, screamed to the end of the dock.

There were a few kids in front of me, and a couple of them succeeded in passing both Zack's and Eddie's marks. The heat was on. I sized up the competition. Soccer players are pretty fit. Some of the smaller and lighter ones could be a threat, I thought. But they might not have the lift. Anyway, it wasn't long before my turn came around again. I decided to forgo the opening yell — it would use up too much precious energy, and I wanted to concentrate on my speed out of the gate.

Focused on Caitlin's hand, I was poised and ready. Her arm sliced the air. I sprang forward, gathering steam. The end of the dock approached. I adjusted my stride. And stubbed my toe.

"Yeowwww!" I screamed. My jump was motivated more by pain than form, as I grabbed my foot reflexively. It was ugly. If I had travelled as far out as I did up, I could have won easily.

Fortunately, the pain subsided quite quickly in the cool water. Zack had hung back, waiting for me.

"You okay?" he asked.

"Sure. No problem," I said, more embarrassed than hurt.

"Check it out," he said, pointing toward shore, off to the right of beach. A few of the kids were jumping off the rocks into the water, under the watchful eye of Steve.

"Looks like fun," I said, glancing at the growing lineup at the dock. "Let's do it!"

The beach ended on the right where a rock face rose about three metres above the lake. The rocky part of the shoreline extended as far as the limits of the camp property. Our cabins were set back in the trees, not too far from where the kids were jumping. At the edge of the beach, a well-packed trail led uphill at a sharp angle into the trees. We picked our way carefully between the exposed tree roots and rocks. A handful of boys and girls, Doug included, were waiting their turn at the jump to leap into the water below.

Doug waved us over. "What's the deal?" I asked him.

"Just take a couple of strides before you jump and remember to keep your arms and legs close. The rock sticks out in the middle. Or, you can go off the left side and drop straight down," he replied. As he spoke, one of the guys ran straight out and over, much like we'd been doing on the dock.

"Piece o'cake," Zack said confidently, stepping into line. The next guy walked cautiously to the edge and leaned over. He stepped back a few paces as though he was going to run, but reconsidered and took the safer route off the side. Zack snickered.

After my little toe-stubbing incident, I was seriously considering playing it safe, but Zack's sneering contempt changed my mind. In characteristic Zack manner, he threw himself into the jump. I couldn't see how far off the rock face he fell, but from the triumphant whoop after the splash down, I could tell he enjoyed the ride.

That was all the push I needed. I ran straight off the rock and let gravity do the rest. It was incredible! When I came up, Steve waved me over. "Good form, kid," he said. "Just keep doing what you're doing." I beamed.

I caught up with Zack. "That is so cool," I said.

"Yeah, he replied, "But I'm getting a little tired. I think I'll take a time-out after my next jump."

"Sure, sounds like a plan," I said. Up to that point, I hadn't noticed how pooped I was.

There was less of a crowd at the top on our second round. I noticed that Zack started his run closer to the edge than I had, probably trying to cut down the amount of energy he needed to propel himself off the cliff. I waited for Steve's all clear. When it came, I took an extra step backward, wanting to be certain to clear the point of rock I'd seen a few feet below the top.

My leap was successful and I landed with a satisfying splash. I followed Zack to shore, swimming just clear of his kicking feet. My eyes caught a flash of something red. I blinked and whatever it was disappeared. Wierd, I thought. Must have been a fish.

Zack was waiting for me in the shallows. "I think I kicked the rock or something," he said, looking down toward his feet under the water. "Maybe not."

We continued on to shore, Zack trudging up the beach ahead of me. I looked down at his footprints. There were dark, reddish spots in the centres of the right ones. "Hey, Zack," I called. "Sit down!"

"What?" he replied, turning back. His eyes followed my pointing finger. "What's that?"

"Your foot, man, check your foot!" My voice was rising in volume.

"Shhh," Zack admonished. He looked around cautiously, and walked a few more feet onto the grass before sitting down. Zack hunched his body over his foot. I dropped to the ground beside him. In the centre of his right foot was an ugly, bleeding gash.

"Holy cow," I hissed. "You're gonna need stitches for sure." I looked around. Steve was still in the water watching the last few jumpers. "I'll get Steve." I started to get up, but Zack grabbed my arm and pulled me back down.

"NO!" he croaked. "It's okay. It's nothing. It'll stop soon."

"I don't think so, Zack," I said, doubtfully. "Remember that time I cut my hand on the barbed wire? It wasn't anywhere near as big as that and I got five stitches."

"I said it's okay, Mitch." Zack's face was dark, and from the way his eyebrows were pulled together in a frown, I was pretty sure it wasn't okay. He caught me staring at him.

"What if they send me home, Mitch? What then?" Now there was something else in his face, fear maybe. He was right, they probably would send him home if he needed stitches.

"What do you want to do?" I asked, as if I didn't know the answer.

"Nothing."

"Right." I had my doubts, but I would never rat on my friend.

6

Blood and Ice

I must have slept like a log, because when morning wake-up came, it took every ounce of willpower I had to drag myself out of bed. My bunkies weren't much brighter, except for Doug, who was one of those annoying morning people you hear about.

By the time we'd straggled to breakfast, Zack, Eddie, and his bunkies were halfway through the meal. I grabbed a tray, loaded it with fake-looking eggs the colour of the sun on the Lone Pine sign, and squeezed myself onto the bench beside Zack.

They were winding up a joke about life in Sycamore cabin, and I had to wait to get Zack's attention. He was looking pretty normal, so I casually inquired about his overall health.

"I'm cool," he replied. I caught his eye and then glanced down to indicate his foot. "Totally cool," he reiterated.

"What's so cool?" Eddie interrupted, to my annoyance.

"Cliff diving," I snapped.

"Yeah, I gotta give that a shot this afternoon," he carried on. The rest of the guys at the table jumped into the conversation, so I gave up trying to speak to Zack privately.

After the meal, we were headed out to the bus when Steve asked for a couple of volunteers to help carry some stuff. Doug and I happened to be walking past him when he made his request, so without waiting for a reply, he steered the two of us toward the kitchen. We each picked up a hamper of lunches and exited by the back door. Steve led us down to the office where he handed me a box of videos.

"Now all we need is the key to the bus," Steve said, stopping on his way out the door to pick a key ring off the Peg-Board. "All set," he said. "Let's go play."

The warm-up was pretty much the same as the day before. I stayed away from Eddie, just in case, sticking closer to Zack. He seemed to be favouring his right foot, but maybe I was imagining that.

When we got to the pylon exercise, I was feeling pretty confident. As usual, I was at the front of the line. My first run went smoothly — all the pylons were in place and I had concentrated on being smooth instead of fast.

While I watched the other kids go through their paces, I noticed, not for the first time, that they were all pretty good. In fact, some were even better than me. I didn't like that much. Together with Zack, I was used to being a top dog on our team. Looking around the arena, I had the sinking feeling that among the thirty-eight other top dogs, some dogs were maybe over the top.

I was considering this unusual situation when Caitlin poked me in the back. "Wake up, Mitch!" she said.

"I am awake!" I replied in a huff, suddenly aware that it was my turn. I bolted into the slalom, but my concentration was off. I toppled the first pylon and before I went much farther, Stan was at my side, whistling me to a halt.

"Mitch," he said, "you forgot the puck." The other kids were killing themselves laughing.

"What?" I said, dumbly.

"We're onto drill number two, go back and start over."

I was totally embarrassed. I guess Stan had called a new drill while I was lost in my reverie. My mind was blank.

Instead of going back, I followed Stan. "Excuse me, uh, Stan?" I stammered. "Maybe you could, like, refresh my memory?"

I'll say one thing for Stan, he was one patient guy. I could see on his face that he wanted to laugh at me, but he repeated his instructions patiently and then skated away.

Keeping my head down so I wouldn't see the looks on the other kids' faces, I headed back to the top of the course and collected a puck. Doing complete circles around the pylons with the puck, was much harder than the S-curves of the day before. The constant shifting of weight and change of direction required all my concentration, so I tried to put my humiliation behind me.

The first time the puck rolled off my stick, I nearly panicked. To retrieve it meant that I would have to deviate from the pattern. Not certain what to do, I took two strides, reconnected with the puck and executed a figure eight to put me back into position for the counterclockwise rounding.

I was smooth, for sure, but not perfect. Caitlin managed to run the circuit without any side-trips. She was pretty cocky when she pulled up behind me.

"What was wrong with you back there?" she inquired.

"Nothing, I just let the puck get away. Could happen to anyone," I replied.

"No, I mean before that. You were just standing there like a zombie."

"I think I have water in my ears," I lied. "I'm having trouble hearing."

Caitlin bought my story. "Maybe you should tell Stan," she suggested.

"Nah," I said, "it'll go away."

"But maybe it's affecting your balance." Boy, that Caitlin was like a dog with a bone, as my mother would say.

"Give it a rest, Caitlin," I retorted. Her face fell and I could tell that she was stung by my remark. Tough. I had problems of my own.

When Stan was satisfied with our progress with the pylons, he moved us over to the face-off area and had us form a loose circle.

"Pick your player, call his or her name and pass the puck," Stan announced, dropping the puck onto the ice in front of his stick. He glanced around the circle, called out "Caitlin!" and snapped the puck over to her. She took the pass with ease and called my name.

Her pass to me seemed to contain some fury, and it whipped right past, between me and the guy to my right. Stan retrieved the puck and sent it back to me. "Accuracy is what we're looking for here, kids." His remark caused Caitlin to blush. "Accuracy at both ends, and a quick release. Let's try again."

I looked around the circle and chose my receiver. My pass was on the money and he took it cleanly. He, in turn, called the next player and released the puck in a perfect demonstration of Stan's instruction. I was impressed. In order to be ready when it came back to me, I decided to pick Caitlin next, but it seemed like forever before anyone passed me the puck. I was beginning to wonder what was going on when I heard my name.

Once again, my attention had been wandering and I had little time to determine the location of the puck before it came over to me. I bobbled it a bit, croaked Caitlin's name and shovelled her the pass. I didn't expect her to send it back to me, and I wasn't ready with my next name.

I hesitated for what seemed like an hour before I came up with a name. After a while I started to relax and the passes became automatic. Then Stan stepped in.

"Let's try a little variation," he said. "This time, I'll call the passes." The puck dropped and I heard my name. Before the puck kissed my stick, Stan shouted "Vince!" I looked around, blindly, forgetting where Vince was. When I relocated him, over to my right, I backhanded the puck, grateful to be rid of it. The action was fast and furious, and I barely had time to scan the circle when I heard my name again.

The puck was pinging between teammates at lightning speed, and we let our reflexes take over. I discovered that I knew, eventually, where everybody was located in the circle, and it was a rare pass that went to the wrong player.

I was grateful when the coaches whistled the end of the morning practice. I sought out Zack, to check on his foot. He was lounging against the boards, waiting to get off the ice.

"How's it going?" I asked.

He glanced around before answering. "It was throbbing a bit during the pylon exercises, but it's cooled down since then." We stood there in silence for a while.

"What do you think of the competition?" I inquired, eager to get Zack's opinion.

"No big whoop. There are some pretty good players, but nobody to give us any grief." As always, Zack was confident, despite his injury. I wished I was as sure of myself as Zack.

† † †

I was exhausted, although my brain probably hurt more than my body. We headed back to the dressing rooms, where I sat down beside Zack. The rest of the players flew out of their skates, but Zack held back until the room had cleared and we were the only ones left.

"Hurry up," I said. "I'm starved."

"Yeah, yeah," Zack replied. "Go ahead if you want."

I walked over to the door, and when I glanced back at Zack, something in his face stopped me. He was grimacing as he pulled his right skate off. I saw the blood first. His sock was soaked with it.

"Zack," I said, "you're bleeding!"

"I was afraid of that," he said. "Mitch, get me a towel, will ya?"

"I better get Stan," I replied, shaken by the sight of Zack's bloody foot.

"No!" Zack said, tersely. "You promised!"

Against my better judgement, I found Zack a towel and stood guard at the door while he cleaned his wound. I watched him rip the towel with his teeth and bind a piece of the cloth to his foot with his hockey tape.

"This is not good," I said, thinking that I really didn't need another thing to worry about. My words were prophetic. In the afternoon skate, I was a total disaster.

7

Camp Clown

After dinner that night, we got to watch a video about the famous 1972 Canada-Russia Hockey Series. It happened way before any of us were born, but it was about hockey and we were keen.

My dad had told me how, when he was just a kid, he and his dad played hooky to stay home and watch the final game on TV.

Steve and Stan rolled a big TV to the front of the dining hall, and the rest of us moved the tables out of the way and lined the benches up in rows. I sat with Zack and Doug in the back row.

Hardly any of the Canadians wore helmets and they all looked pretty old, compared to hockey players now. Some of them were losing their hair, just like my dad. And they sure looked tough compared to the Russians.

Back in the olden days, only Canadians played in the NHL, not like now, so even though some guys on the Canadian team played in the United States, they could still be called Team Canada.

"How come it doesn't say 'Russia' on their shirts?" someone asked.

"It does," replied Stan. "That's what the letters CCCP mean. Actually, they mean Soviet Union, which is what they called themselves then."

I don't think there was anyone in that room who didn't know that Canada won the series, but a lot of what we saw was news to us. The video showed parts of each game and we cheered the Canadians and booed the Russians just like it was happening right there and then.

We recognized some of the guys' names because they're still around, but boy, they sure looked different. A lot thinner, for certain. And their clothes were hideous. Something else I noticed — when they interviewed the Russians, they were all really polite.

About halfway through the video, at the point where the Canadians went over to Russia to play, it showed them all being introduced at centre ice. When Phil Esposito stepped forward, he fell flat on his butt.

"It's Mitch Stevens," Eddie shouted, raising a howl of laughter from the crowd.

I was glad the lights were out, because the way my face was burning, it must have been flaming red. Trust that big jerk Eddie to get his laughs at someone else's expense. A few seconds later they showed Esposito waving and laughing down there on the ice. A Russian player said something about admiring his style and I felt a little better, especially since Esposito was such an important member of the team. I guess there are worse things than being compared to someone like that.

The truth is, when they played at home, Team Canada stunk. It wasn't until they got to Russia that things turned around. I found myself on the edge of my seat, wondering what it was like for Dad to watch it happen for real.

When Paul Henderson scored his goal, everyone in the room leaped to their feet, cheering wildly. There was more tape on the video, but we weren't watching.

Finally, Stan brought us to earth with his customary whistle.

"We've got a little video of our own, here. Sit back down and enjoy the *Camp Lone Pine Great Plays and Dismal Bloopers of the Century*."

The video opened with a shot of the ugly sign, then cut to a shot of the bus. The doors opened and kids streamed out. They kept coming and coming, maybe a hundred or two. More than the bus would hold, for sure. The last bunch of kids included Zack and me. Judging from the T-shirt I was wearing, it was shot the day before.

There was a series of excellent plays, in which former campers scored goal after goal. They showed us working our drills both yesterday and today. It was all casual until the bloopers started. They began with a shot of me draped over one of the cones. I had been clowning around, pretending to get hung up on a pylon. But on video I looked like an idiot. I guess the other kids agreed, because they laughed loudly.

I noticed that Zack wasn't in any of the bloopers, nor was Eddie. Doug was featured lying on his back in the net, one skate stuck in the netting. But there was no doubt who the star of the bloopers section was. It was me.

I had had a terrible afternoon, and there it was on the screen, in living colour. The video showed me skating toward an open goal, in the clear, close enough that a sneeze would have sent the puck into the net. And I shot it wide. Not a little wide. Way wide.

There I was again, skating across the blueline, when invisible ice gremlins just reached up and pulled me down. And finally, as if all that wasn't enough, the video showed me standing by the door, waiting to leave the ice, and I fell again.

"Hey, is that Phil Esposito?" Eddie shouted. "Sorry. It's just Mitch Stevens again."

My face hot with humiliation, I got up, mumbling about having to go to the bathroom. Actually, I didn't want to face my mates when the lights went on.

I wandered over to the recreation centre. The soccer players were watching World Cup of Soccer videos, but I'd had
my fill of videos.

Soon I found myself down by the lake. Walking to the end
of the dock, I removed my runners and dangled my feet in the
cool water.

If the coaches had set out to humiliate me on purpose,
they couldn't have done a better job. Was I really lame? I
wondered. And why didn't they just send me home right now?

My reverie was broken by the sound of something whiz-
zing by my ear, followed by a series of plopping sounds. I
looked around as another object splashed down a few feet
away. It was dark, and I couldn't really make out the identity
of the person on shore. Whoever it was, they sure knew how to
skip stones on the water.

I picked up my shoes and headed to shore to investigate.
The stone-skipper rooted in his or her pockets. As I got closer,
I recognized him.

"Hi, Doug," I said.

"Oh, hi Mitch," he replied. "I didn't see you out there."

We stood there for a few seconds. Doug held a flat stone
in the palm of his hand. He lightly tossed it up and down.
Finally, he took it between his thumb and forefinger and with
a gentle flick of his wrist, sent it out across the water. The
stone disappeared from sight but the sound of three skips was
distinct. Plink, plink, plink, plop.

"Here," Doug said, holding out a stone to me.

I took the stone and tried to imitate his motion, but it
splashed down only a couple of metres from the water's edge.

"It's all in the wrist," Doug said, demonstrating for me.
He handed me another stone out of his pocket and this time I
succeeded in making it skip once before it submerged.

"Got another one for me?" I asked.

"All out," Doug replied. "There's more over there." He pointed toward the trees, where the water had undercut the shore. I put down my shoes and waded over to the spot he indicated. He followed me. In the shallow water, tons of small stones were piled against the shore.

"Here, you want smooth ones like this," he said, handing me a flat, disk-like stone.

We collected a bunch more, filling our pockets. Once again, we returned to the sand at the water's edge.

"How about that video, eh?" I inquired, as casually as I could.

"The Russian thing?" he replied.

"No, the other one."

"Yeah, I was thinking maybe I would go back there tonight and destroy it," he said, echoing my own thoughts.

"It wasn't so bad for you," I said. "I was the blooper king."

"How many?" Doug asked.

"Four," I replied.

"Yeah, you win," he said. "Three for me."

I must have missed Doug's other two bloopers.

"I think mine were worse," Doug continued. "I ripped the net, scored against my own side and that last thing, I think I broke their camera."

I laughed. "Good, maybe they won't take any more videos."

"Yeah, maybe we're both blooper kings!"

The next stone I tossed skipped at least five times.

8

Minor Improvement

After my little chat with Doug, I knew I wasn't the only one afraid that I wouldn't make the cut. But Doug wasn't here with a best friend who wouldn't hear any talk of failure. Zack was so completely confident in his abilities, *and mine*, that the idea of failure wouldn't enter his head.

But Zack was afraid of something else. What was worse? Being sent home because of a cut on your foot? Or being cut from the team? We could end up home together, for entirely different reasons, and I bet Zack would never look at me the same way again. Suddenly I'd be a loser. He'd only be a hotshot who had a bad break. Crazy thoughts like those had me ready to throw myself in front of a Zamboni.

On the other hand, it was only day three of hockey camp and that meant I had ten more days to shine. In other words, today was the first day of the rest of camp. Time to get out of my head and into my game.

* * *

I ran into Zack on the way up to the bus. He was coming out of the infirmary. I waved him over.

"How'd it go?" I said, assuming he had been to see the nurse about his foot.

"Okay," he replied.

"Don't you need stitches?" I asked.

"I went to ask for some aspirin, Mitch. That's all."

"Oh." I got the feeling Zack didn't want to talk about his foot. "For your foot?"

"No. I told her I had a headache so she would give me some aspirin. Let's drop it, okay?"

Boy, Zack was getting testy. And when Zack was testy it was best to just shut up or talk hockey.

"Doug says we're actually going to play a game today," I said.

"Yeah? Where'd he hear that?" Zack's attitude did a one-eighty.

"He knows somebody who was here last month and they split into teams on day three and played a full game."

"It's about time," Zack replied. My news cheered him up, because he picked up the pace. I was certainly looking forward to a few shifts on the line with Zack — and getting some of the old magic flowing again.

"Yeah, just what the doctor ordered," I said, laughing. "Take two face-offs and call me in the morning!"

I couldn't wait to get my skates on. Of course, we had to go through the usual aerobics on ice. Fortunately, there weren't any pylons in sight.

Doug was right about the game. After our classroom session, the coaches met us on the ice. Stan had his clipboard and, piled on the ice on either side of him were red and blue vests. Zack and I checked them out as we skated past. "Cool," Zack said. "Game time."

Stan called out our names and told us which colour to pick up. I was relieved that Zack and I were both on the red team. However, I was not so pleased when Eddie joined us.

Once we were all assigned and had our vests draped over our jerseys, one of the kids on our team yelled out "Team Canada!" We took up the name with great enthusiasm, taunting the blue team. They didn't want to be Team Russia, but it was too bad. The name stuck.

Brian Epstein started in goal for us, and it wasn't long before he was being called Esposito — Espo, for short. We tried to remember the names of the other players on the old Team Canada, but we could only remember a few, and everybody wanted to be Henderson, even the defence players. Steve put an end to the discussion.

The game started with me at centre, and Zack and Caitlin on wing. I could see that Eddie wasn't too happy starting the game on the bench, which gave me a sudden desire to score on the first shift.

I met Doug in the face-off circle. "Hey, Boris," I said. "Welcome to Canada!" I said it like the Russians did, *Kaw-naw-daw*. Doug laughed, the puck dropped and he took the face-off. "Oops," I said aloud, as I skated after the action.

Fortunately, Zack was able to quickly gain control of the puck and the play moved into the "Russian" end. I took a pass from Zack who was being swarmed by blue defencemen in front of the net, but I was driven wide by another blue defender. We hit the boards together and struggled for a piece of the puck.

There were more blue flies coming in for the kill. I managed to kick the puck off the boards and it dribbled around behind the net. It took an enormous effort to get the blues off me, but I did, allowing me to set up to the left of the crease.

Zack was behind the net, spinning and twisting in the narrow space, teasing a blue player as he controlled the puck. I saw his shoulder dip. Here comes the deke, I thought. I was locked hip-to-hip with another pesky blue fly, but I readied myself, alert to the clues in Zack's body language.

Sure enough, Zack faked out the blue girl on his tail, sending her one way while he slid the puck around the net in the opposite direction, where I waited for a rebound.

It was a good move, but their goalie — nicknamed Tretiak after the famous Russian player — pounced on it with his glove. Through the mask, I could see Tretiak's look of triumph. But as he opened his glove to toss the puck back into play, the look turned to surprise. Nothing came out.

He wasn't the only one expecting the puck to land outside the goal crease. The blue fly at my side had unfastened himself in preparation for the new play. My eyes locked on the black disk snuggled up against the goal post, mere millimetres from the magic line.

Out of the corner of my eye I could see the goalie's head snap around, but it was too late. All it took was a tiny tap from my stick and the puck was where it belonged. One score for Team Canada. Take that, Eddie, I thought smugly, as my teammates crushed me to the ice.

We held the Russians off for most of the first period, but when they scored, seconds before the buzzer ended the period, it was during my shift. I shovelled the face-off to Caitlin who carried it to the blueline, deftly escaping the pursuing blue players. She dropped a perfect pass back to me, and without thinking I broke the first rule of hockey, skating across centre ice with my head down. Duh! I took a check out of nowhere, losing the puck to a blue, who drove through our defence like a knife through butter. Espo made him work for his goal, but he was relentless with the rebounds.

For the second period, Steve made some lineup changes that included replacing Caitlin with Eddie. I wasn't too happy about that, but Zack seemed to welcome the switch.

When Zack, Eddie and I took to the ice for our first shift together, I noticed another change. Zack was slowing down. Where he had dominated the play during our shifts in the first period, Zack seemed to hand the second period lead to Eddie, apparently content to cruise, playing point for Eddie and me.

Although it disturbed me, I had to admit that the unspoken arrangement had its benefits. Zack would attach himself to the side of the net, letting us work the puck end to end. We were down by one goal, midway through the period.

The play was in the Russian end for most of the shift, with furious activity around the net that was handled admirably by the blue team's Tretiak. Then the puck was cleared to our end and we hustled to get onside for a new attack. Eddie took the puck from one of our girls on defence and began the drive. Zack skated straight out and back in, taking up his now familiar position to the right of the goal.

Eddie had the puck, coming up the right side. He spun around a blue man and released the puck to me on the left. I was being driven toward the boards when I saw Eddie had a reasonably clear shot. I dumped it to him and moved into position to the left of the net.

The drive was thwarted as a blue defenceman sacrificed himself on the ice at Eddie's feet. "Eddie!" I shouted, and before the word had left my lips, the puck smacked solidly onto my stick. I didn't need radar to know that Zack was waiting by the net. I pivoted, sliding the puck with me as I made the snap shot to Zack. It was over in the blink of an eye: from Eddie, to me, to Zack, to the net.

I was loving it. I had to admit we made a great threesome, and for once, Eddie had grudging praise for me. Not that I needed it, not from him. But it was an improvement after all those digs.

It was pretty disappointing, when, in the next period, Steve shifted things around again and Zack wound up on a different line. I was doubly disappointed that Zack was replaced by Caitlin. With her superior skating skills, Caitlin was capable of outshining me, and I was way more comfortable with Zack's style of teamwork.

On our first shift together, it was obvious that Eddie avoided passing the puck to Caitlin. It wasn't very smart team playing, and when the shift ended, Caitlin confronted him about it.

"What's the matter with you?" she demanded of Eddie. "We're supposed to be playing as a team. I'm on your line, you pass to me. Simple." She headed back to her place on the bench. While her back was turned, Eddie made faces at her, mouthing the words, "blah, blah, blah."

"I saw that, Eddie," Caitlin said, wheeling around. She stomped back and stuck her face up close to his. "You got a problem with girls on your team?"

I cringed when Caitlin said that. The fact is, most of us guys aren't that comfortable with girls on the ice, especially tough guys like Eddie. Of course, nobody, including me, would admit it. Caitlin could sure hold her own in an argument. Meanwhile, Eddie just stood there grinning at her like a dumb ox. Caitlin headed down the bench for a second time.

"Sit down, Eddie," Steve called out. "And next shift, let's see some *teamwork*."

While all this was going on, I was watching Zack's line. He hadn't changed his strategy from the previous period, only on his new line, he didn't have the support of the other two players. They kind of worked around him, and as he left the ice at the end of his shift, he looked completely beat. I couldn't help but think it was obvious to Steve and the other coaches.

"You okay?" I whispered as he sat down beside me.

"Headache," Zack replied loudly enough for Steve to hear.

"Right," I said, with a knowing look. Probably the best way to play it, I thought, hoping that Zack's "headache" would miraculously clear up overnight.

In the meantime, we had work to do if we were going to break the tie. It was during the dying minutes of the third period when Eddie, Caitlin and I stepped into the fray. Caitlin clearly had plenty of energy, as she demonstrated the skating skill that must have earned her the right to be here.

She was in the right place at the right time, taking a deflection off a skate and putting it upstairs for the go-ahead goal. At least, that's what they told me. I was face down at the blueline at the time. I dusted myself off and joined my teammates.

"Way to go, Caitlin!" I hollered over the crowd.

"Call me Henderson," she said.

9

Night Crawlers

For the first time in a while, I actually felt energized after the day's workout. I left Zack at his cabin, still loudly complaining about his "headache," and continued on down to the beach. As usual, the soccer slackers were already there, which led me to wonder how hard they worked each day, compared to us.

A couple of nets were stretched across the sand, all set for beach volleyball. I looked around for the counsellors, eager to get in on the action. A stream of kids was heading toward a clump of campers at the farthest net, so I joined the parade.

I was assigned to a mixed team, meaning there were both soccer and hockey players on the side. It made it a little confusing, because I didn't know the soccer players' names.

Playing volleyball on sand is pretty tricky, so it's a good thing we all had strong ankles. Even so, I fell a few times on the churned-up powder. The counsellors gave us their usual warning about being careful not to hurt ourselves, which made me think of Zack. I looked around and didn't see him. It was probably just as well, because he couldn't play in bare feet.

The game was a lot of fun, but I wasn't very good. The harder I tried, the worse I got. It was okay, though, because my antics were a hit with the crowd. On the few occasions when I actually returned a volley in the right direction, I ran around the court pumping my fists in the air like Rocky Balboa. I was pathetic. It was great.

On the way up to dinner, I stopped in at Sycamore to look for Zack. He was dozing on his bunk.

"Hey, buddy, wake up," I said. "It's supper time."

"I'm not hungry," Zack replied, a look of pain on his face.

"Does that mean you're not coming?" I asked.

Zack grunted in reply. I took that for a "no" and headed for the door. I looked back at Zack on the bed and asked, "Do you want me to bring you something?"

"More aspirin," was all he said.

I didn't want to miss dinner, but I was pretty worried about Zack, so I stopped in at the office to ask if the camp nurse was still around. The director, Mary Skorsgaard, looked like she was about to leave as I barged in. This was the first time I had seen her since the day I arrived.

"Hello, young man," she said, peering at me like I was a bug or something. "What may I do for you, this evening?"

Wow, I thought, I wonder if she's always that polite? Suddenly, I couldn't remember why I was there. While I noodled it out, she continued to stare at me with icy alien eyes.

"Oh, yeah!" I said, brightly. "Is the nurse around? My friend Zack has a bad headache. He needs some aspirin or something."

Mary put the bag and keys she was carrying down on the desk. "A headache?" she said. "Does your friend often have headaches?" She sat in the chair and wheeled herself over to a file cabinet. "What's his name?"

"Zack Andermann," I replied with sudden panic, afraid she was going to call Zack's parents.

Mary pulled a folder out of the drawer, and opened it on her lap. "Nothing in the file about headaches." Snapping the folder closed, she said, "This sort of thing happens sometimes, with the extremes in the temperatures. I'll have a look at him. The nurse has gone home."

Oh great, I thought, just what I didn't want to happen.

I followed her out of the office, trotting along behind her as she strode, very briskly, down the hill toward the lake and Sycamore. She glanced back and, seeing me behind, slowed down a bit. "Why don't you go up to dinner, young man," she said, not unkindly.

"Mitch," I said. "I'm Mitch Stevens."

"Of course, hello again, Mitch. I remember meeting you with your parents on your first day of camp."

"If it's okay I'd rather go with you. I'm kind of worried about Zack," I added.

"Well, aren't you a good friend," she said brightly.

Sure, I thought, let's just hope Zack thinks so when I show up with you.

As we neared Sycamore I picked up the pace, eager to alert Zack to Mary's impending arrival. I scooted ahead of Mary and announced, in what I hoped was a natural voice, "Zack! Mary's here to look at you!"

What a dweeb! I paused at the door, holding Mary at bay. Mary reached around me and knocked on the door. "Zack, it's Mary Skorsgaard. May I come in?"

"Yes," Zack called out weakly and we entered. He played the headache thing to the hilt, and when Mary commented that he felt feverish, he blamed the heat. By the time Mary left us, Zack had his aspirin and I had major hunger pains.

I convinced Zack to join me, and we both headed up to the dining hall where the staff was clearing up the remains of dinner. The cook took pity on us and prepared a couple of plates of leftovers, but when I was finished the meal, I was far from full.

There's nothing worse than going to bed on an empty stomach, which was exactly what I did that night.

It tormented me and when I couldn't take it anymore, I woke Doug up.

"Got any food?" I asked, as he grumbled in annoyance. "I'm starving. I missed dinner."

When Doug was fully awake, he announced that he too was hungry. Our conversation awakened the others, and we determined that there was no food to be had in Alder. "We can order a pizza. Got any money?" Doug asked.

"Some," I replied. "What about you?" While we figured out how much money we would need, one of the guys piped up, "How you gonna order pizza? You don't have a phone."

"There's a phone in the office," Doug reminded them.

"How you gonna get in?" asked Mr. Logic.

Doug and I looked at each other. "We'll go through the doggie door," I said, remembering the hinged flap in the door that I'd seen the day we arrived.

The other two guys looked at us like we were crazy. "It could work," Doug said. "Come on, Mitch."

On the way up to the office, we made a detour to Zack's cabin, figuring that if I was hungry, he must be too. I snuck in the door and crawled over to his bunk. Tugging on his sleeve, I whispered, "Zack, wake up." By the time Zack woke up, there wasn't anyone left sleeping in Sycamore.

We took to the night again, now with Zack and Eddie in tow. We darted through the trees, pretending to be soldiers on our secret pizza mission, dodging imaginary bullets.

We gathered in the shadows of the office wall and peered in the windows. The coast was clear. "The phone is on the desk to the right of the door."

"Okay, who's smaller," I asked, "me or Doug?" Zack and Eddie sized us up and announced in unison, "Mitch." That made me it.

"Right," I said. "Doug, you're from Huntsville, who's got the best pizza?"

We all looked at Doug. "Call, five, five, five, seven, seven, seven, seven," he said in reply.

"Are you sure they'll deliver all the way out here?" Zack asked.

Doug grinned, his teeth white in the darkness. "My sister works there. She told me they stopped offering the thirty-minute-or-free guarantee because it's too far, but they still deliver pizza."

"Ready, Mitch?" Zack asked.

I duck-walked over to the door. "I'm going in!" I announced.

I got onto all fours like a dog and poked my head through the flap. Eddie and Doug got behind me to help. I sniffed the air inside, like a dog. Twisting my upper body, I angled my shoulders into the opening. For some reason, I didn't put my hands through first and got myself lodged in the opening.

"I'm stuck," I announced. Doug and Eddie muttered at me, as they each took one of my legs. They lifted me off the ground.

"Push!" Doug said, and they gave me a heave. Instead of popping me through the opening, they caused the door to swing open with me still wedged in its bottom. Doug and Eddie fell into the entrance, forcing the door against the wall behind it. My head hit the wall with a thud.

"Oww!" I hollered. The two guys dropped my legs like a sack of potatoes, but I was still wedged in the doggie door as Doug sat down to dial the pizza place.

"What do we want on our pizza?" he asked.

While Doug gave our order, Zack and Eddie released me from the door. With that part of the mission accomplished, we settled down to wait for our food.

"Somebody better go up to the road to intercept the driver," Doug suggested, and we agreed that it wouldn't be smart to have the car pull into the camp.

He volunteered and I offered to accompany him. Closing the office door, we left our two companions behind the dining hall and headed for the road.

We walked along in silence for a few minutes, until we reached the big ugly sign.

"Where do you play in Toronto?" Doug asked, out of the blue.

"Everywhere," I replied. "We play all over the city."

"There's pretty good teams there, eh?" he said.

"Yeah," I answered, not sure of where he was going with his questions. "Some, like our team, the Hillcrest Stingers, and Eddie's team, the North York Rangers, are really good."

"What about Scarborough?" he asked.

There were a couple of guys at camp from the Scarborough Devils. They were good too. I told Doug what I knew about them and he fell silent again.

"I'm moving to Toronto," he said, out of nowhere.

"What?"

"My mom and my sister are packing while I'm at camp and we're moving to Toronto as soon as I finish."

"Hey, man, that's cool," I said, but something in his voice made me think that it wasn't so cool for him. Then I found out why.

"My folks are splitting up. I have to go with my mom," he said.

I didn't know what to say to him. I just stood there on the side of the road, kicking the gravel.

"Do you think I'm good enough for the Toronto leagues?" Doug asked.

I had an answer for that one. "You bet, Doug," I said honestly. "You've got nothing to worry about there."

When the car with the illuminated pizza sign slowed to a stop in front of us, I was as grateful for the food as I was to end that particular conversation. I didn't want to get any deeper into who was good enough for what. With only ten more days left at Camp Lone Pine, my bad start hung over me like a dark cloud. Instead of concentrating on making the select team, I was worrying about being cut.

10

Dog Day Afternoon

It was the best pizza of my life, and I've had a lot of pizza. Not just because it tasted good, which it did, but because I ate it at hockey camp, in Muskoka. For those few minutes, I forgot about Zack's foot, my ice follies, Eddie's teasing and everything else that had or could go wrong.

Of course, the feeling didn't last. I have no idea what time we made it back to bed, fanning out through the trees like jungle hunters, stalking imaginary prey. Judging by the way I felt when morning came, it was really, really late.

Zack and Eddie were dragging their behinds up to breakfast like two snails on a teeter-totter. "Hey, pizza boys!" I said, greeting them on the path.

"Mmm," mumbled Eddie, his hat on sideways, as he concentrated on the path at his feet.

The conversation at breakfast didn't get much better than that. Our energy was completely focused on eating.

By the time we finished breakfast, I was ready for a nap, so I took full advantage of the thirty-minute bus ride to town. As I stepped off the bus, Caitlin gave me a funny look.

"What's with you guys this morning?" she asked.

"What guys?" I replied, baffled.

"There were four of you flaked out in the back of the bus, snoring up a storm," she announced.

"Get out!" I retorted. "Kids don't snore."

"Yeah, well, he does," she said, pointing at Eddie. I howled with laughter, sorry I hadn't been awake to hear that for myself.

Caitlin wasn't the only one giving us weird looks. Stan and Steve gave us the eyeball as we stumbled onto the ice. We were barely into the warm-up and I was already feeling like I had two left skates.

I groaned inwardly when Stan announced that we would be concentrating on power skating. Great, I thought, why can't we just stand around in a circle and whip pucks at each other all day? But my wish was not to be granted.

By the end of the skating drill I knew how to fall down very well. They had us practically dancing on the blueline, prancing like horses. It was evil.

Agility and balance were what Stan wanted from us. I looked around the ice and saw a fair bit of clumsiness, especially among the midnight pizza patrollers. Only Caitlin managed to stay on her feet throughout.

I was very happy when the focus changed to deking, passing and shooting. I think best with a stick in my hand.

My heart leaped with joy. It was my old favourite, the two-on-two drill: two forwards against two on defence. We split into two groups for the drill, starting at centre ice, working opposite ends. My first pairing was with a girl I'd played against in Toronto.

I carried the puck across the blueline and faked a shot to my partner. The player opposing me was fooled. I was clear for a shot on net, but the point of the drill was to pass the puck so, reluctantly, I sent the other kid a wrist shot. I was impressed when she swatted it out of the air, but her opposing defender came up with it and cleared it toward the blueline. Without thinking, I raced across to the other side to get it, but my partner was already there, leaving nobody to receive my pass.

Embarrassed, I rushed toward the net, eager to set myself up for her pass. The defence wasn't taking it sitting down. They played me like a guitar, making me fight for the ice room. My partner's shot was high and right on the net. The player to my left threw himself in front of the shot and it slammed down onto the ice a few paces ahead of me. I lunged for it, stretching and sweeping my stick to clear the puck around the player lying on the ice.

With the puck now behind the defenceman, and nothing else between it and the net, I straightened up, shifted my weight to my back foot, dragged the puck to the front and flicked my stick. The puck popped off the surface and headed for home.

A black glove shot out and robbed me of my goal. Brian Epstein grinned behind his mask. "Got it!" he said.

"Thanks for the news flash," I replied, feeling a little testy. I skated back to the redline thinking I'd have to do better if I wanted to make the impending cut.

Of the four pizza patrollers, only Doug managed to score. Zack was lame in more ways than one, and we sleep-skated our way to lunch.

The most energy we exhibited all day went into taking off our equipment and heading outside into the sunshine where we flaked out on the grass. Within minutes, we were asleep. An annoying drone intruded into my dreams, and I awoke to the sounds of laughter.

When I opened my eyes, Caitlin and the five other girls were gathered around my head, peering down at me. I sat up abruptly.

"Wake up, Sleeping Ugly," Caitlin commanded. Her friends giggled. "It's time for school."

Jumping to my feet, I rushed to wake my sleeping companions. I shot an angry glare at Caitlin's departing back, thinking that she was getting a little too confident after her big goal yesterday. She was right about one thing, though. Eddie did snore.

We straggled into the classroom, taking seats at the very back. The session was already under way, and my hopes for a sleep-inducing video were dashed when Stan started asking questions. At least once he caught me with my mind wandering.

After class, we hit the ice for a two-period game. We kept the same teams as the day before, which made it easier for us.

The game gave me my second wind. Back on the line with Zack and Caitlin, I muffed the face-off. When Zack didn't chase it, I went after it myself, plucking it off the stick of a blue forward. The three of us steamed toward the blueline together. I had the puck going into the zone. My pass to Caitlin was wide, picked up by a blue defence player, who cleared it out of their end.

We swung around, back to the play. One of our defencemen was scrambling along the boards, leaving the other one alone to defend. We weren't fast enough to stop a blue forward from taking the puck in against our man. I saw it as if it were in slow motion, the blue man lifted his stick, took a short backswing to draw the defenceman and the goalie, then quickly changed gears, pivoted and placed a clear shot at an open net. It should have been me. Wrong end, wrong goal.

We lumbered off the ice. "Stinky, huh?" I said to no one in particular. Zack sniffed.

"I'm bagged," he said. "D.O.S. Dead on skates."

"Better not let Steve hear you say that," I said, under my breath. "We haven't exactly been greased lightning today."

"No kidding," he agreed. "And my foot is killing me. Power skating was the last thing I needed."

I conserved my energy between shifts, because on the ice I felt like I was skating for two. I hated to admit it, but we needed Eddie out there with us. Caitlin just wasn't strong enough to compensate for Zack's lack of energy.

We got my wish for the second period when Steve switched the lineup again. We were better than the first period, but still not up to our performance of the previous day.

I won the face-off in our end, and passed the puck to Eddie. We started the march to the other end, Eddie and Zack skating up the boards on opposite sides, with me bringing up the rear.

Eddie reached the blueline with the puck a few steps ahead of Zack. He passed the puck across the ice, along the blueline where Zack picked it up. He was occupied by blue defenders along the boards, allowing me time to reach the net. Zack freed the puck, dropping it back to one of our defencemen. The teammate flicked one up to Eddie, who was driven off the puck.

I chased after it, before the blue man could get a chance to clear it. We wound up on the ice and my stick got fouled up in his gear. By the time we got clear of each other, the play was at the other end. Wearily, I dragged myself to our blueline, prepared to wait forever for the puck to come my way.

I didn't have to wait long. Eddie fired one out to me from the corner. I wheeled around, overjoyed to see a solitary blue between me and glory.

I summoned my hidden reserves and angled in for the shot. But it was not to be. I fanned it.

"What's the matter, Stevens?" Eddie cackled. "Puck too hot for you?"

My retort, which would have been brilliant, died on my lips as Eddie chased after the opposing player who had scooped the puck from me.

11

Trouble Afoot

At the end of the game, there was a lineup to get off the ice, so Zack and I hung back waiting for the traffic jam to clear.

"Hurry up, I'm freezing out here," Zack complained in the general direction of the door.

"How can you be?" I said. "You just finished a shift."

"I don't know," he replied. "Maybe they turned on the air conditioning."

We were practically the last guys off the ice and I knew we were in trouble when I saw Eddie and Doug standing uneasily behind Stan, outside the dressing room door. Stan waved us over. I shot Doug a "what gives?" look, but he just shrugged and hung his head.

"Somebody like to tell me what's going on here?" Stan demanded. His question was met with four blank expressions, mine being the blankest of all.

"In one day you go from being four good players to four mediocre players. Somehow, I don't think it's a coincidence that it just happens to be you four. Now, I'm going to ask again, and this time, I'd like an answer." Stan paused for effect. "What's going on?"

A hundred thousand things went through my mind, as I struggled to come up with a plausible explanation for our lacklustre performance. The truth wasn't one of them.

Unconsciously, I cleared my throat, and found four pairs of eyes riveted on me.

"Mitch?" Stan inquired. "Care to enlighten me?"

"Oh," I said, clearing my throat again, stalling for time. "Yeah, well, you see, we were hungry." I paused, trying to figure out if we could be charged for breaking into the un-locked office. I looked around, but there was no help forth-coming from my co-conspirators. They appeared as interested in my story as Stan was.

"Yeah, so, um ... " I had a flash of brilliance and before I could consider the consequences, the words tumbled out of my mouth. "We all ate these cookies my mom sent, and they made us sick."

"That's it?" Stan said. "Why didn't you say something this morning. Did you throw up?" He looked at each of us in turn. We nodded. "Do you have any of the cookies left?"

I panicked.

"No, sir," Doug piped up. "We threw them in the kitchen garbage bin this morning."

"Yeah," Eddie piped up. "They were pretty awful."

"Hey," I protested, glaring at Eddie in defence of my mother's imaginary cookies. "They tasted fine. Maybe we just ate too many of them."

"All right, fellas," Stan said, waving us toward the dress-ing room. "Please, if you have any more problems, if you feel sick or hurt yourself, tell me immediately. Got it?" We nodded in agreement. "Okay, let's get out there!"

I was relieved to have dodged that bullet, but I still had an uneasy feeling that I was turning into the camp weasel. I'd lied to camp staff two days in a row. I was helping Zack hide his injured foot. Somewhere up there was a lightning bolt with my name on it, waiting for me to do one more sneaky thing, then kaboom! Struck down in my prime.

It was a quiet ride home, especially since four of the biggest jokers were struck mute by guilty consciences. Zack huddled in the seat, his warm-up jacket pulled tightly around him.

I knew I sounded like a broken record, but I had to ask. "You okay, Zack?"

"Yeah, I'm just cold," he said. "It'll pass. I guess I shouldn't have had that cold pop."

Doubtful, I thought. Zack's face was red and shiny with sweat. When we got back to camp, he excused himself, complaining of a stomachache.

Back in Alder, after dinner, Doug and I had a long discussion about the meaning of "good" in Stan's comment about "four good players." Did that mean good enough to make the cut? Stan didn't say great, or excellent, or stellar, words *I* would have used. All that pondering made me sleepy, so I turned in while the lights were still on.

I was sound asleep dreaming that we were shooting cookies instead of pucks when I was awakened by something clutching at my sleeve. The cookies morphed into something human at the same time I opened my eyes.

"Arggh!" I bellowed. Eddie's face hovered over me in the moonlight.

"What's going on?" Doug muttered, half asleep.

"Nothing," I replied. "Go back to sleep." I swung my feet onto the floor, stuffed my feet into my shoes and dragged Eddie outside.

"Are you nuts?" I demanded, thinking that Eddie was pulling some juvenile prank intending to embarrass me.

Eddie didn't answer, he just pointed to a human form huddled against a tree.

"Zack!" I rushed over to my friend. Even in the dark, it was obvious that Zack was in trouble. In the moonlight, his face glistened with sweat, but it was ghostly pale and his lips were grey.

"He started moaning and babbling a little while ago. The only thing he said that made sense was your name, so I brought him." Eddie peered at Zack over my shoulder. "What's wrong with him? Do you think it's the cookies?"

I looked at Eddie in amazement. "Eddie, there never were any cookies, remember?"

He grinned sheepishly. "Oh yeah, I forgot."

"Listen, Eddie, you better go back to your cabin. I don't want you to get into trouble, or anything."

"Yeah, okay. If you're sure." Eddie got to his feet. He took a last look at Zack and turned back down the path.

"Eddie!" I called after him. "Don't say anything about this, okay?"

"No problem, Mitch. Anything for a friend."

I wished I had longer to ponder the contradiction in his words, but Zack grabbed my head and pulled my face right up to his nose.

"Hospital," Zack croaked. "You gotta … me … hospital, Mitch."

He was scaring me. "I should get the camp director, Zack," I said, rising to my feet.

"NO!" Zack shrieked.

"Shhh!" I looked around for lights to come on in nearby cabins, but the camp remained still. "This is crazy, Zack. I can't get you to the hospital. I don't know where it is and besides, I can't drive."

Zack shook his head, as if to clear the cobwebs. He peered intently at me.

"We could call a cab," I suggested, realizing immediately that we could never pay for fare all the way to Huntsville.

"Pizza," Zack said cryptically, lapsing into his feverish babble.

"How can you think about pizza at a time like this?" I demanded, annoyed.

"Pizza drive us to town," he mumbled.

"Oh," I said, "not a bad plan, except we spent all our money on last night's pizza."

I couldn't believe I was having this conversation. "Zack, I'm going to call an ambulance. I think they're free."

Instead of answering, Zack clamped a soggy paw on my bare arm and glared wildly into my eyes. "No noise. No one must noise."

Great, I thought, that leaves the bus. The good news was that I knew where Steve kept the keys. The bad news was that we were going to die on the way to the hospital. Sometimes friendship can be a killer.

I dragged Zack up the hill, convinced that we were both off our heads. In the moonlight we cast long shadows that looked like walking trees. The bus sat between us and the office. I pulled open the door and helped Zack aboard. Stepping off the bus, I prayed that my arcade driving experience would help me pull this off.

Inside the office, I was relieved to find the keys hanging on the Peg-Board where I'd seen them before. I reached up to take them when the realization hit that this was the sneaky thing that would bring the lightning bolt down squarely on my head.

I fell into the chair behind the desk, drumming my fingers on its wooden surface. As I pondered my fate, my nervous digits strayed along the blotter and started tapping the phone keys. "Call 911," said a voice in my head that I recognized as my mother's. "Wake the camp director."

"NO NOISE!" shouted another voice, a strangled Zack-sounding voice. I looked around. I was alone. "You promised!" came the voice again. Goosebumps raised up on my bare arms.

Zack was my best friend. How could I betray his trust? We'd already had a terrible fight this year, and maybe it wasn't about life and death and feet, but it was big and tested our friendship. But what if Zack was really sick? What if they amputated his foot? It may already be too late!

"Pick up the phone, Mitch," another voice said. I looked around again, before I realized it was my voice. I was talking to myself. I lifted the receiver and let my fingers do the walking.

"Dad?"

"Mitch? Mitch! What's wrong?" Dad's voice went from sleep to panic in one note.

"Um, nothing." Oh, duh! Like I would call in the middle of the night to say hello. "Actually, Dad," I said, "I've got a little problem. It's about Zack."

As if on cue, the door banged open and Zack stumbled in. I levitated two, maybe three feet into the air. "What time ... mother ship?" Zack demanded.

"Houston, we have a problem," I said into the phone.

"Is this some kind of a prank, Mitch?" Dad asked, annoyance creeping into his voice. In the background I could hear my mother murmuring.

"No, sir," I sighed. "I wish it were." I laid it out for him, sparing no details. Well, maybe I left out the part about Mom's cookies. Zack was content to wait for the mother ship, oblivious to my conversation on the phone.

"Do you know where to find the camp director?" Dad asked.

"Mary? Yeah, I think so. I definitely know where Stan is," I replied.

"Good, go get one of them now, I'll wait on the phone. Bring them back with you."

I dropped the phone on the desk and tore out of the office without a moment's hesitation. It wasn't until I got Stan back to the office and onto the phone with my dad that I considered how bad it must look for us being in the office so late at night. At that point, all that mattered was getting Zack looked after.

Stan hung up the phone. "Give me a hand with him, Mitch," he said, crouching beside Zack who was now dozing. We lugged Zack out between us. "We'll take my car. It's behind my cabin. Your fathers will meet us at the hospital."

"Yes, sir," I said.

When we got to Stan's car, a Ford Taurus, I went to open the back door, but Stan stopped me saying, "Let's put him in the front seat, so I can belt him in. We don't want him to roll onto the floor in the back."

"Okay," I said, helping Stan arrange Zack in the front. He tilted the seat back a little, so Zack wouldn't flop forward. I climbed into the back and fastened the seat belt.

The trip to Huntsville was as quick as Stan could safely make it. He made frequent checks on the dummy in the front seat. The dummy in the back seat was silent the whole way.

12

Truth and Consequences

What a night! My dad must have called my Aunt Barb, who lives in Huntsville, because she was there waiting for us in emergency. They took Zack into an examining room and made me sit outside. It was brutal waiting while Stan and Aunt Barb conferred with the doctor.

When they finally came out, they confirmed what I had feared — Zack's foot was badly infected and he had a high fever. Aunt Barb and I sat down to wait for Dad and Mr. Andermann, while Stan took off in search of coffee.

They must have driven really fast, because they showed up in record time. Aunt Barb took Mr. Andermann to where Zack was sleeping, and Dad sat down beside me. I was ready for a blast of parental disapproval, but he just asked me how I was doing and settled in to wait.

I must have been dozing because I didn't see Mr. Andermann come back. He tapped me on the shoulder and said, "Would you like to see Zack now?"

I bolted from the chair, not waiting for anyone to accompany me. When I arrived in the room, Zack was sitting up.

"I screwed up," he said. I was relieved to hear that he was talking normally.

"Yeah," I replied. "We both did."

"Nah, you just did what I asked." He leaned back on the pillows again. "I just hope you don't get into trouble for it," he added.

You and me both, buddy, I thought, watching his eyes close. Within seconds he was fast asleep, so I snuck a peek at his foot, under the sheet. The cut was covered in bandages, so I still didn't know if he got stitches.

I wandered back to the waiting room. Dad was alone. "Ready to go, champ?" he asked.

"Where is everybody?" I said, dumbly.

"Barb's gone home, and Zack's dad has gone to the pharmacy. Zack's going to have to stay here in emergency until later this morning, then we'll take him back to Toronto."

Zack's worst nightmare was coming true. "Are they kicking him out of hockey camp?" I asked with alarm. I didn't wait for Dad to answer. "Are they gonna kick *me* out?"

"Zack needs to stay off his foot for a while," Dad said. "Why don't we go get donuts? And I need a coffee." Dad didn't wait for me to answer, he just headed for the door. As he passed the desk, he had a few words with one of the staff. I followed, my stomach churning. I didn't need a donut, I needed answers. If Dad wasn't saying, it was because the news was bad. I was doomed — Dad was trying to soften the blow with an orange cruller.

* * *

It took all of thirty seconds to drive to the donut shop which reminded me that the last time I saw Stan he was going for coffee. "Where's Stan?" I asked, thinking he was probably back at camp, packing my gear.

"He left while you were sleeping." The parking lot was full of cars, people were heading to work and lining up for their morning coffees. Dad took the keys out of the ignition. I didn't want to hear my fate in front of all those strangers.

"What did he say, about Zack and me? Are we toast?" I demanded.

Dad had the door partly open. He turned to look at me, then closed the door again. "Why do you think you're 'toast'?" he asked.

"Because we messed up. We lied about Zack's foot," I answered.

"Did you lie?" he asked.

"Well, yes," I stammered, "but it was to protect Zack. I just said he had a headache." Dad didn't need to know about the imaginary cookies.

Dad sighed, one of those big, "I am so disappointed in you, I could expire right here" sighs. "You're not getting kicked out of camp, Mitch," he said. My heart leaped in my chest. But he wasn't finished.

"You're right. You both messed up. But it was an error in judgement, not a malicious act. If you'd done something on purpose, to hurt someone or to damage something, that would have gotten you kicked out for sure. In this case, you both made some wrong assumptions and they could have had dire consequences for Zack. Remember that hockey player who nearly died because of an infected scratch? That's the sort of thing that could have happened when you both let Zack's cut go untreated."

The queasy feeling was back in the pit of my stomach. Flesh-eating disease. That's what dad was really talking about. I shuddered. "I wanted him to see a doctor, Dad," I exclaimed. "Really, I did. He begged me not to tell. What was I supposed to do?"

"Sounds like your instincts were correct, Mitch. You should have followed your gut feeling. I understand your loyalty to Zack. What I don't understand is why you didn't think you could call me. It helps to get a second opinion. And you might have saved Zack a lot of pain and discomfort."

"We were afraid they'd send him home," I answered in our defence, nervously opening and closing the glove compartment.

"Even if they did, Mitch, Zack could still have returned to camp when he was better. Don't you think his dad would have done everything possible to help him?"

I guess we hadn't thought of that. Dad opened his door again. This time he got out of the van. "Oh ye of little faith," he said, cryptically. "And I thought we were friends." He gave another super sigh and waved me along behind him.

"We are," I hollered, scrambling out of the car after him. I had another matter to discuss with my "friend."

Dad ordered a large black coffee, orange juice and a maple donut. I joined him in the orange juice, choosing a big apple fritter *and* an orange cruller for myself. We sat at a table in the non-smoking section, and ate in silence for a few minutes.

I practised a few opening lines in my head, not wanting to sound ridiculous. Finally, I settled on an approach.

"What happens if I don't make the cut?" I blurted.

Dad took a sip of his coffee. "You go home and it's business as usual," he said, evenly.

"And if Zack does?" It was something that haunted me daily.

"It will take a lot of strength to accept that, but it's the risk you both took coming to camp," he replied, looking me in the eye. "It could go the other way too, Mitch."

I hadn't thought of that. And now, with Zack out of commission, maybe for the rest of camp, it was a real possibility.

"Did you ever think you weren't good enough?" I asked, getting to what was really bothering me.

"Every day," Dad said, surprising me. "Keeps me humble."

"I mean, when you played hockey, were you ever afraid you'd be cut from the team?"

"Of course, Mitch," he said. "That's what made me work harder. Besides, I could see I wasn't the best. I worked at being as good as *I* could be. Not to be better than somebody else."

"Did you ever screw up?" I was thinking of the blooper video, how I looked like a fool.

"Are you kidding?" Dad laughed. "I don't like to tell this story, because it was probably my most embarrassing moment on ice. There I was, finally playing for a team that people paid real money to see. My first game. I checked my gear a thousand times. I put my stuff on in the right order. The stands were full when we marched out of the dressing room. The announcer called my name and I boldly skated onto the ice. And fell flat on my face! I'd forgotten to take my skate guards off!"

I laughed so hard I spit orange juice all over the table. Now that's a blooper, I thought. Must run in the family.

Dad looked at his watch and stood up. "Time to get you to the arena."

"Right," I said, with more enthusiasm than energy.

We pulled up to the arena behind the camp bus. Dad stopped the van, but didn't get out. He extended his hand and we shook, man to man. "Remember, son, leave those skate guards in the dressing room."

I laughed again, and hopped out of the van. The door was closing as my dad said, "Mitch? Should I ask your mom to make you some more cookies?"

With a wicked chuckle, he drove away.

13

Making Up for Lost Goals

Dad and Zack's father drove back to the city, and Zack went home with them to recuperate. I was lost without my pal, feeling guilty that I still had a chance and maybe he didn't.

You can imagine my elation when I saw Mr. Andermann's van pull into the lot four days later, around dinner time. My joy turned instantly to horror when I saw Zack hobble out, using his hockey stick as a crutch.

I ran to meet them, confused and afraid. Suddenly, Zack tossed the stick into the air and started dancing crazily around the lot.

"You're a madman, Zack Andermann," I said, punching him hard on the shoulder.

"You got it, Mitch. Madman on skates. Take me to your arena!" he said, laughing.

The next morning, Zack was the first player on the bus. He had been told to take it easy, but I knew Zack, and that was impossible. I decided to keep an eye on him myself, and blow the whistle if he appeared to be hurting. Better safe than sorry.

Eddie had been almost as happy to see Zack again as I had. "I can't wait for us to get back on the line together. We make an awesome team, right, Mitch?" he exclaimed. While Zack was away, Eddie had spent most of his time with Doug

and me. But the insults didn't stop, and Eddie seemed oblivious to their effect on me. One day, I asked him why he did it.

"What do you mean?" he answered. "I'm just joking
around. It doesn't mean anything."

I wasn't about to tell him it bugged me, and after that
conversation, it didn't.

We hit the ice like tornadoes, anxious to get through the
drills and into the meat of the day ... the game.

While Zack had been gone, Stan shuffled the teams a
little. Eddie and I were still on the red team. Doug had joined
us from the other side, and we were the top-scoring line. Zack
stayed on the red team with us, but he was on a different line
for the first period. No matter. We were playing for the same
side.

Right from the opening face-off, I could feel the adrenalin
pumping. It had become a point of honour to score on the first
shift. We won the face-off, and within seconds, Eddie was
steaming toward the blue goal. His drive was blocked by two
determined blue men. He spun around in anticipation, and
backhanded a pass to me as I came up behind him. While
Eddie occupied the blue defenders, Doug was setting up in
front of the goal, preparing for my pass.

Sticks were poking at my feet, and I could hear the heavy
breathing of an opponent giving chase. They were driving me
hard, past the point where I wanted to unload. I could hear
Doug shouting, as the boards rushed up to meet me. The blue
flies that had been picking at me had already bailed, leaving
me a fraction of a second before impact to pass to Doug. I
made the suicide pass, and went straight into the boards at full
speed watching as I went down to see that the puck found its
mark.

Doug deflected the puck at the net. It was stopped by the
blue goalie who planked it right back at Doug. He'd been
spun by a blue player, and his stick wasn't on the ice when the

puck came out. Meanwhile, Eddie executed a wide sweep to the right of the goal and was making a fresh approach as Doug kicked at the puck with the skate. He succeeded in putting the puck out of reach of the blue player beside him.

Eddie screeched to a halt directly in front of the goal and hammered one through. Goal!

I was still shaking my brain back into position when I joined the celebration. "Somebody better check that goalie," I said. "I think he has a puck-sized hole right in the middle of his chest."

We left the ice, setting up the challenge for Zack's line to match our effort. His linemates were Caitlin and a centre named Vince. Caitlin was a speed demon — she could skate rings around most of us — and paired with Zack, she would have plenty of goal-scoring opportunities. All the centre had to do was win the face-off and watch those two dominate the play.

Their first face-off went to the blues, who wasted no time in peppering our goalie with shots. Zack finally forced the blue defence away and picked off a rebound to send the puck to their end.

Icing was called, and the line set up for another face-off. This time, our centre did the job. Zack had the puck and hovered around, waiting for everyone to get onside. He broke out of the holding pattern, crossing the blueline with Caitlin and the centre abreast.

He took a swing, just inside the blueline. It was a beautiful slap shot that rebounded to their defence. The defence fanned the shot, giving Caitlin a golden opportunity to score. Her shot was true, but the goalie stopped it, and swept the puck around behind the net where one of his forwards was waiting.

Zack thundered back there, driving the blue girl off. He bounced the puck off the side of the net, taking his own rebound. He couldn't make a shot on the goal, so he fired the puck out to one of our teammates on the point. Vince's shot rebounded into the hands of the opposition and their drive for our end began.

Our players in the end were on the ball, intercepting the puck and sending it out to the blueline where Caitlin waited. It was one-on-one. Caitlin blazed up the middle, outrunning the competition behind her. The lone defender was caught too far to the right and pumped like mad to catch her. In a valiant, but futile attempt, he threw himself and his stick into her path.

Caitlin lightly backhanded the puck behind her, out of reach of the prone defenceman, and then she jumped neatly over his stick.

Zack screeched in to pick up the pass, carving a V around the stick man. With a sweet little snap shot, he snuck the puck between the goalie's legs.

What a team! Zack parked it on the bench beside me, glowing with pride. "I think we're gonna make it," I said quietly, not wanting to appear overly confident.

"Of course we are," Zack replied. "Did you doubt it?"

"Actually, yes," I said, honestly. "There are some really good players here."

"Yeah, and we're two of them," he answered.

I looked at Zack, wondering if he ever had a moment's doubt about anything. Probably not. And if he did, it wasn't Zack's style to admit it. He was one hundred percent positive energy.

"Still," I said, "we're lucky we didn't get ourselves kicked out of camp."

Zack looked at me soberly. "Yeah," he said, "I nearly messed it up for both of us. I owe you, Mitch." We sat quietly, watching the game for a few more seconds. Then he said, "When we make the select team, I'll let you score the first ten goals."

That's the spirit, Zack, I thought. *When*, not *if*. "When we make the select team," I announced, "I'll score the first *twenty* goals, *unassisted*."

"When you guys are ready," Steve interrupted, "there's work to do." The shift was changing once again.

I never worked so hard in my whole hockey life, as I did those two weeks at Camp Lone Pine. Zack went back to Toronto with a scar on his foot. I left with a new attitude.

Did we make the team? Well, that's another story.

Other books you'll enjoy in the Sports Stories series...

Baseball

☐ *Curve Ball* by John Danakas #1
Tom Poulos is looking forward to a summer of baseball in Toronto until his mother puts him on a plane to Winnipeg.

☐ *Baseball Crazy* by Martyn Godfrey #10
Rob Carter wins an all-expenses-paid chance to be batboy at the Blue Jays' spring training camp in Florida.

☐ *Shark Attack* by Judi Peers #25
The East City Sharks have a good chance of winning the county championship until their arch rivals get a tough new pitcher.

Basketball

☐ *Fast Break* by Michael Coldwell #8
Moving from Toronto to small-town Nova Scotia was rough, but when Jeff makes the school basketball team he thinks things are looking up.

☐ *Camp All-Star* by Michael Coldwell #12
In this insider's view of a basketball camp, Jeff Lang encounters some unexpected challenges.

☐ *Nothing but Net* by Michael Coldwell #18
The Cape Breton Grizzly Bears face an out-of-town basketball tournament they're sure to lose.

☐ *Slam Dunk* by Steven Barwin and Gabriel David Tick #23
In this sequel to *Roller Hockey Blues*, Mason Ashbury's basketball team adjusts to the arrival of some new players: girls.

Figure Skating

☐ *A Stroke of Luck* by Kathryn Ellis #6
Strange accidents are stalking one of the skaters at the Millwood Arena.

Gymnastics

☐ *The Perfect Gymnast* by Michele Martin Bossley #9
Abby's new friend has all the confidence she lacks, but she also has a serious problem that nobody but Abby seems to know about.

Ice hockey

☐ *Two Minutes for Roughing* by Joseph Romain #2
As a new player on a tough Toronto hockey team, Les must fight to fit in.

☐ *Hockey Night in Transcona* by John Danakas #7
Cody Powell gets promoted to the Transcona Sharks' first line, bumping out the coach's son who's not happy with the change.

☐ *Face Off* by C.A. Forsyth #13
A talented hockey player finds himself competing with his best friend for a spot on a select team.

☐ *Hat Trick* by Jacqueline Guest #20
The only girl on an all-boys' hockey team works to earn the captain's respect and her mother's approval.

☐ *Hockey Heroes* by John Danakas #22
A left-winger on the thirteen-year-old Transcona Sharks adjusts to a new best friend and his mom's boyfriend.

☐ *Hockey Heat Wave* by C.A. Forsyth #27
In this sequel to *Face Off*, Zack and Mitch encounter some trouble when it looks like only one of them will make the select team at hockey camp.

Riding

☐ *A Way With Horses* by Peter McPhee #11
A young Alberta rider invited to study show jumping at a posh local riding school uncovers a secret.

☐ *Riding Scared* by Marion Crook #15
A reluctant new rider struggles to overcome her fear of horses.

☐ *Katie's Midnight Ride* by C.A. Forsyth #16
An ambitious barrel racer finds herself without a horse weeks before her biggest rodeo.

☐ *Glory Ride* by Tamara L. Williams #21
Chloe Anderson fights memories of a tragic fall for a place on the Ontario Young Riders' Team.

☐ *Cutting it Close* by Marion Crook #24
In this novel about barrel racing, a talented young rider finds her horse is in trouble just as she is about to compete in an important event.

Roller hockey

☐ *Roller Hockey Blues* by Steven Barwin and Gabriel David Tick #17
Mason Ashbury faces a summer of boredom until he makes the roller-hockey team.

Sailing

☐ *Sink or Swim* by William Pasnak #5
Dario can barely manage the dog paddle but thanks to his mother he's spending the summer at a water sports camp.

Soccer

☐ *Lizzie's Soccer Showdown* by John Danakas #3
When Lizzie asks why the boys and girls can't play together, she finds herself the new captain of the soccer team.

Swimming

☐ *Breathing Not Required* by Michele Martin Bossley #4
An eager synchronized swimmer works hard to be chosen for a solo and almost loses her best friend in the process.

☐ *Water Fight!* by Michele Martin Bossley #14
Josie's perfect sister is driving her crazy but when she takes up swimming — Josie's sport — it's too much to take.

☐ *Taking a Dive* by Michele Martin Bossley #19
Josie holds the provincial record for the butterfly but in this
sequel to *Water Fight* she can't seem to match her own time and
might not go on to the nationals.

☐ *Great Lengths* by Sandra Diersch #26
Fourteen-year-old Jessie decides to find out whether the ru-
mours about a new swimmer at her Vancouver club are true.

PRINTED AND BOUND
IN BOUCHERVILLE, QUÉBEC, CANADA
BY MARC VEILLEUX IMPRIMEUR INC.
IN SEPTEMBER, 1998